THE PURPOSE

by

JOSHLYN RACHERBAUMER

WHISKEY CREEK PRESS
www.whiskeycreekpress.com

Published by
WHISKEY CREEK PRESS
Whiskey Creek Press
PO Box 51052
Casper, WY 82605-1052
www.whiskeycreekpress.com

Copyright © 2013 by *Joshlyn Racherbaumer*

Warning: The unauthorized reproduction or distribution of this copyrighted work is illegal. Criminal copyright infringement, including infringement without monetary gain, is investigated by the FBI and is punishable by up to 5 (five) years in federal prison and a fine of $250,000.

Names, characters and incidents depicted in this book are products of the author's imagination or are used fictitiously. Any resemblance to actual events, locales, organizations, or persons, living or dead, is entirely coincidental and beyond the intent of the author or the publisher.

No part of this book may be reproduced or transmitted in any form or by any means, electronic or mechanical, including photocopying, recording, or by any information storage and retrieval system, without permission in writing from the publisher.

ISBN: 978-1-61160-589-1

**Cover Artist: Ester Rose
Editor: Marsha Briscoe
Printed in the United States of America**

Dedication

To my very own prince charming, Chris. God has blessed me abundantly to love you eternally.
Until then…

Chapter 1

Winter

The door slammed, shaking the walls and caging Audrey into the darkest moment of her life. A picture of Jason fell near her head. The crash of broken glass released all of her internal fear and she collapsed to the floor in a fit of rage and tears that felt like they would never end. Sobs erupted from far deep inside her and she only came up for air when August rammed his stubborn little head against hers.

"He left, love. He is never coming back," she muttered into his black fur. "You think we will be okay?"

Audrey lay on that cold, fake laminate floor for three and a half hours until finally she crawled across her pitiful apartment and tumbled into bed. This is where her sister found her two days later.

"You have got to be kidding me, Aud! You should

The Purpose

be thanking God that he left. You never had the audacity to kick him out yourself and I know you never would have," Emma said as she bounced on top of the mound of covers surrounding her sister. "I fed your stinking cat; what a great mother you are."

"Oh buddy." Audrey poked her head from underneath her sister, looking for August. "I should just die. At least he would have a better owner who would feed him."

"Okay, here is the plan. Get your smelly butt out of bed and shower. When you are done, we are going for a walk and eating some lunch. Baby steps will lead you to recovery," said Emma and smiled, a little too brightly. "Oh and one rule, you don't even say his name…not once!"

Audrey groaned and slumped off the bed. If you knew Emma, you would know how relentless she was and there is no point in fighting back. Crawling to the bathroom floor, she turned on the hot water and peeled her clothes of two and a half days from her weak little frame. Weight loss would hopefully be a silver lining from this deep depression. Her sister was obnoxious, but as always, right. She melted under the blasting strength of the water and imagined it washing away all of her sadness. Although the thought of her sadness made tears drip down the shower drain again, she pressed on until she eventually reached for a towel. It was twenty-five minutes of delightful warmth and although she felt exhausted, a bit of fresh air sounded sinful.

Walking across her apartment in the best outfit she could muster, yoga pants and a sweatshirt, she burst into tears again when she spied the broken frame on the floor. Emma leapt in front of her and forced her in the opposite direction.

"I will take care of that. Right now, focus on getting out the door."

As Audrey sat on the walkway trying not to fall over, Emma moved quickly to clean up the glass. After inspecting August's paws for any damage, she locked the door behind her and stopped in her tracks at the site of her tragic sister.

Audrey had slumped over on the concrete with blonde curls surrounding her face. The cool winter air was beginning to pick up and although it had yet to shoot down snow or ice this season, the sky seemed to be getting grayer by the day. She slipped some mittens on Audrey's frail hands and lay down next to her. Holding her face in her hands, she wiped her tears away and put her nose to hers. Audrey's laughter erupted from the dark hole inside her heart as Emma's eyelashes fluttered against her cheeks.

"You always know how to make me laugh," said Audrey and sighed.

"Hey, you started doing *eyes* to me when you were little and you think I would have let it go by now, but great things never die. There is something so hysterical about the way your eyes look when our faces are smashed together; guaranteed giggle maker," Emma said in return. "Now get up and let's walk it out!"

Begrudgingly, Audrey stretched her legs and set out on a long soothing stroll. Emma's arm linked in hers, she started to breathe again. The distraction of the crispy fresh air and the crunchy leaves underfoot reminded her of the snowfalls to come. There wasn't a moment to remember Jason and, even better, the grief of her life. It was as if Mother Nature was determined to breathe life into her once again. They walked along in silence, lost in the beauty of the gray skyline and jagged sticks that used to be flowing trees. There wasn't a season Audrey didn't love and there wasn't a chance for a walk that she would turn down. The tears didn't come even once during their dance around the neighborhood, and despite her best efforts, Audrey couldn't feel sad. Maybe there was life after tragedy after all.

Chapter 2

Spring

Eyes closed, Audrey relished in the moment. Never believing she would see this day, it would be impossible not to feel as if someone would snatch it away from her. *Just breathe*, she told herself. She had been telling herself that for months. First it was simple things like remembering to eat. Gradually, more complicated moments took the place of the simple, like mustering up the courage to meet her friends alone. Surprisingly, her work and education suffered minimally during her depression, but then again she had always been a people pleaser.

After Jason left, she fell far down into a bottomless pit. Emma kept telling her the day she hit rock bottom would be the day she would remember forever and start climbing her way back out. Maybe Emma could have been a little more descriptive; otherwise Audrey would have seen it coming.

The Purpose

She had thought for so long after he left that the moment the door slammed was her rock bottom. Wrong. There is not a class out there that prepares you for the gut-wrenching phases of grief. This initial moment had merely been the start of countless episodes of self-blame, loneliness, deep depression and finally the most aggressive version of herself she has ever known. Currently in the angry phase, she found herself needing to find a way to get the sweetest form of revenge. She found the opportunity at *Handle's*, the safe haven of her recent days, a bar not even a quarter of a mile from her house.

Sulking in the corner with Emma and vodka and diet soda, a double, she was mid-chew on her ring finger when her sister reached across the sparkle-filled granite table top and smacked her hand with vengeance.

"What in the hell?"

"Knock it off. I have decided I am going to beat you into stopping that disgusting habit. You have no idea how irritating it is to see you eating your hands," forced Emma.

"You haven't smacked me that hard since we were kids fighting over video games. What in God's name has gotten into you?"

"You. Quit sulking and let's order some food."

Emma reached for a menu and focused with such an intensity to avoid the glare she was getting from Audrey. Bar food; was there anything greater? French fries piled in cheese, mini cheeseburgers or hmm….maybe hot wings.

"Who's disgusting? How can you even consider that junk? It only clogs your arteries." Audrey grimaced at the images of dancing chicken wings on the table advertisement.

"Tonight is not the night; I have had more than enough of your judgment."

"Wow," said Audrey, clearly amused.

An entirely too bouncy server giggled her way to their booth. If she had been looking across the room at the faces of her future customers, she would have approached with a different expression.

"Welcome to Handle's!" she said and beamed, looking up from her server's book. Her face dropped as she finished her sentence. "I am Serenity?" She seemed to question herself.

"Oh God," moaned Audrey as she slammed her head onto the table.

"Excuse my sister, she is pissed at the world," Emma said and smiled. "Okay, we will start with cheese fries and a salad with ranch dressing for sour puss."

Life was instantly instilled into the little waitress and she assured them of the best service. "I will definitely try and turn that frown upside down!" She bounced off into the bar lights, thankfully before hearing Audrey's snide remark.

On her second bite of the tasteless lettuce, Audrey felt a chill. Her senses had heightened back to super normal since entering the *angry phase* and she was far too in touch with her surroundings.

"He is here," she gasped.

"Who? Oh my God, where?" Emma swirled around in her booth, frantically scanning the room. "He is at the

The Purpose

hostess stand…with…I can't see! Move little Serenity! Ummm…" Emma was practically falling out of the bright red booth to the floor. "A girl; oh my God, don't look. She is not exactly attractive and….he has her arm around him. I will get Serenity and pay and we will get the hell out of here," insisted Emma in one seamless breath as she searched through her purse for her wallet.

Audrey sat stunned. She had been waiting for this moment for months. She had imagined what she would say. Something along the lines of, "You have no idea what you lost because you never had me. Thank you for leaving; you did me a huge favor. My life is beyond perfect now and the only time I ever think of you is when I laugh to myself, imagining how pitiful making love to you was," she would say with such confidence. She would get every single word out before flipping her freshly highlighted hair in his face and prancing off in her newest pair of sexy kitten heels.

Now, here she sat in the food-filled booth with nothing even remotely similar to her imagination other than having had her hair done last week. However, now it sat in a messy up do that was falling out of the clip as she sat horrified. Every bit of confidence she had dreamed of escaped her like a deflated balloon when a child shoves a tack into it. She was paralyzed, picturing his face in hers, screaming the day he left. Her makeup was surely smudged from rubbing her hands up and down, demonstrating her impatience with Emma. She was lost without her signature look of brightly colored shadow and a sweeping liquid liner in a cat-eye swirl. Covered head to toe in clothes that were too big for her, a sweatshirt and gym shorts that hung low like a basketball player, she looked hideous. There was absolutely no way she could let him see her; not like this.

As Emma ran for the waitress, Audrey unglued herself from the bench and slid slowly downward. The red booth seemed to mock her as she attempted to wedge herself underneath the table only to hit her head; not once, but twice. At five feet seven inches, she was tall and gangly. Mid-squeeze, she realized the severity of this idea. She started to cramp and panicked. The only thing worse than him seeing her at all was seeing her like this. Finally, she felt her bottom bounce off the concrete and braced for whatever pathetic situation was to come.

Here on the sticky bar floor with a French fry permanently attached to her leg, it dawned on her what her sister had been talking about. *This* was her rock bottom. There was no denying how pitiful it felt to have your head cocked sideways, squished under a gum-encrusted table bottom, knees drawn to your chest as your feet slipped around on the greasy floor. Audrey could see his every move from her pitiful position. She watched painfully as he escorted her with his hand on the small of her back to a seat across the room. She watched as he laughed his deep enthusiastic laugh at his new girl when she spoke.

Emma had lied. She was beautiful and vastly different than anything Audrey would ever be. She had short, mocha-colored hair with soft pale skin. She was much shorter than Audrey, easily by three or more inches with heels. And oh God, her heels! They were sky-high in a cheetah print that

The Purpose

only accented her perfectly sculpted calves. Her skirt was mid-length but hugged her hips like a cat woman suit. She had a lacy top that revealed a camisole underneath and several pieces of sharp silver jewelry hanging from her ears, wrists, neck and even her ankle. Damn she was sexy; something Audrey had never felt. Audrey dipped her head into her knees and felt the wetness of her tears hit her thighs. How was he with someone so fast? She hadn't even entered the *Miss Independent* phase of her grief and he was already onto the *Dating Someone Else* phase?

Perhaps it was because he walked out on her, but they lived together for over nine months. Doesn't that count for anything? How do you forget someone that fast? What was humiliating was the fact that she had even come to terms with his leaving. She even went so far as dropping to her knees and thanking God for the blessing in disguise. He was wrong for her, she knew that. Then why did this hurt so badly? She scooted out from under the table when his back was to her and ran like the wind out the front door, tripping over the doormat. Emma came running out behind her and found her kicking his tires.

"Well, you're lucky he isn't sitting near a window," mocked Emma. "Let's get out of here."

The entire way home, Audrey recounted his and her every step. Her mind flashed back and forth between the images she had just seen and the memories from their entire relationship. She had loved him as if she didn't love strong enough, he would die, or maybe she would die. There was a deep and troublesome passion to their relationship that she

The Purpose

couldn't describe to anyone. When he kissed her, even the day before he walked out, it shook her to her core. If that wasn't love, she surely would never know what is.

Emma was stone cold silent as she opened the passenger door. Audrey heaved herself out and made her way to her apartment. Nearly two months after he left her and she was back at the beginning.

"Rock bottom," she muttered, slamming the door behind her.

* * * *

Now sitting with her eyes closed as excited chatter surrounded her, she waited patiently, feeling each breath rise and fall within her chest. *Just breathe.* And then suddenly, booming over the audio system came, "Audrey Landrow, Bachelor's Degree in Non-Profit Management, Cum Laude".

She opened her eyes, a smile spreading across her face. The wind picked up and the aroma of the flowering crabapple trees passed over her. She squinted in the sun and walked up the stairs to the stage. Professor Doyle reached for her hand and squeezed with extra strength.

"Well done, my dear." He smiled through his white mustache. "Now go change the world."

"Yes, sir," she said and beamed.

Posing for her picture, she could hear her parents and Emma screeching from the audience. *This is what it feels like to make your parents proud*, she thought. She lifted her dark blue gown slightly and tiptoed down the stage. Making her way through the crowd, although she wasn't supposed to quite yet, she didn't stop until she reached her dad's arms. Tears were brimming over his round cheeks and her mom leaned in to wrap her arms around the both of them. Next came Emma barreling though with a bigger smile than Audrey could ever remember her wearing, squeezing her so tightly it made her square cap fall to the ground.

"I am so proud of you, sis. You did it all by yourself."

The next few hours flew by as Audrey hugged one aunt after another. Congratulations and bear hugs were followed by mouthfuls of chips and dip, fried cheese, veggies and cupcakes, tartlets and chocolate covered candies. Her mother had truly outdone herself with this party and although Audrey had tried to convince her she didn't need it, she realized walking in how much she really wanted it.

Her parent's house sat in a low valley overlooking fields of greenery. Gorgeous spring flowers and huge weeping willows lined the driveway to the Landrow Mansion; at least that was what Audrey called it anyways. It stood almost two and a half stories tall, grazing the white clouds drifting above. The mansion was equipped with six bedrooms, four and a half bathrooms and a special den for her mother's bookkeeping, with hardwood floors that stretched the length of every room. Room height windows let the spring sun come spilling through the panes. Fresh bouquets of tulips and lilies filled every room, making it feel as if the season was changing from within.

The home felt exceptionally too large for the people who lived in it, but now, as floods of extended family filled the driveway to celebrate Audrey's "Coming Back to Life

The Purpose

Party", or rather her graduation party, it was the perfect size. Her mother had a banner made that stretched the length of the kitchen, issuing "Congrats Audrey-Bear" and food towered over the black granite counter top. Her mother had even hired a three piece concert band for inside the house and a DJ for the patio. The violin was Audrey's favorite as it smoothed her nerves from the highly-anticipated afternoon. The guests wore spring dresses, shirts and ties and freshly polished shoes. Although the Landrow family wasn't overly wealthy, everyone knew their events were sure to impress.

When no one was looking, Audrey slipped across the open field to her favorite place in the world. The hidden pond held a flowing fountain in the middle and had elegantly placed stone benches around the edges. If the sun poked between the trees just right, a rainbow would shine down through the center of the water. Overgrown lily pads spread like a stretching hand from one side to the other and in the evening hours, large-bellied bull frogs could be seen hopping clear across the water as if they were dancing to the song of the crickets. Shaggy willow trees swayed in the breeze and a hint of jasmine filled the air. This was what Heaven must be like, Audrey had decided as a little girl. She would take a stack of books or lined paper and a pencil and scribble away for hours beneath the trees. It was here she first decided to write a book, but somewhere in-between the episodes of her own personal soap opera; she had buried that dream among so many others.

Finally alone, she let her head lean back on the bench

and rested her eyes. She studied the various sounds of the birds in the trees and imagined they were singing only for her. She hummed along as she drifted in and out of consciousness.

"Nice song." Will nudged her feet over and took a seat.

"Hey, I was rather comfortable", Audrey scorned, sitting upright. "Although, I guess it is typical behavior from you."

"I have been thinking about you lately," he said knowingly.

"Oh?"

"Yeah, trying to figure out how on earth you of all people could go into non-profit work."

"What is that supposed to mean?" She couldn't help but feel defensive.

"I don't know, I guess as kids I always saw you as the suit on Wall Street type. Ambitious, you know?"

"Really? I would never imagine myself that way. I am way to idealistic and filled with compassion for such a life," she fired back.

"Hey, there is nothing wrong with the corporate world. You just grew up to be the opposite of what I expected, that's all."

There was something about Will. He could rip you apart or build you up within five seconds. Audrey held his glance as he spoke, but couldn't help but feel intimidated. Ever since they had gone their separate ways as adults, these rare occurrences of brief visitations left her speechless to his criticism.

The Purpose

His dark curls fell above his eyes and he swatted them with frustration.

"Forget it," he mumbled. "You never get what I am trying to say."

Another criticism.

"Wanna skip rocks?" he asked in a bi-polar fashion. Leave it to Will to pretend like the previous words were never spoken. "It's either that or find your way to the dance floor; my father has been searching for you for the last hour."

"Sure."

Will searched frantically through the mounds of pebbles to find the perfect one. He held them up to the bursting sun to examine every angle before adding them to a stack he was building next to the pond. Audrey, on the other hand, grabbed any rock with color to it. It never mattered whether they were smooth or flat. She only wanted to be a part of the unique stones. She managed a few across the pond before Will's tall figure shaded the sun from her view. Without speaking, he reached for her hand, removed the stone she was holding and replaced it with a dark gray, perfectly oval pebble.

"Try that one," he said and smiled.

If it had been anyone else forcing her against her will, she would have tossed it and grabbed hers back. Will was being kind and she knew it. This was a rare moment and she intended to cherish it. She hurled the stone with precision across the rippled turquoise water, exhaling a loud puff of air. The stone bounced and bounced until it hit the other side of the pond and Audrey squealed in delight. It had been ages since she had been capable of this feat.

"See, you are accomplished." He grinned, slapping her on the back.

Same old Will, same old pond; some things never change.

* * * *

Smoothing her white lace dress and adjusting her oversized pink Gerber daisy in her hair, she headed back to the party. Will was right, she realized as she could see his father Mark scanning the crowds for her. The dance floor was jam packed with overly excited Landrows grooving to the sounds of their generation. Audrey attempted to weave her way in and out of the crowd to avoid Mark, but low and behold he started shouting over the band for her. She had always danced with Mark as a little girl and was happy to do so. He made it very clear how much he loved his only son, but Audrey was the daughter he always wanted. Their similar mansions backed up to each other and her glorious pond was the merger of their properties. Hours upon hours had been spent weaving through the wooded area to Will's house where they would concoct plans, such as building a canoe for the pond or attempting to find a star in the sky no one had ever seen before. Will started out as a best friend, a brother, and the older he became, the more he distanced himself.

They had spent every day together as children, but high school marked the end of their friendship affair. Her junior

The Purpose

and his senior year, he did manage to be there for her as a homecoming date. Her long time crush, Kyle Adams, begged her to go with him only to ditch her the day before. Audrey hadn't spoken to Will in months, other than the occasional passing in the halls. When he heard the news, he showed up at her back door to make sure she still had a dress. He never asked if she wanted to go with him or even possibly had another date, but instead said he would be there at six in a monotone and with an irritated gesture. Audrey sensed his father had something to do with it, or maybe Emma, but she didn't turn him away. There was no way on earth she could go to homecoming alone after Kyle ditched her.

They had spent the evening standing awkwardly by one another as their friends giggled and swayed to the music. An hour into the dance, he finally asked her if she wanted something to drink and two hours in said he liked her dress. She remembered attempting to inch a little closer to him with each song, hoping he would get the point. She only wanted to dance to make Kyle jealous, but Will was busy on his cell phone. Finally, with a passive-aggressive undertone, she looked him square in the eye and said through gritted teeth, "Will Michaels, ask…me...to…dance." Either she scared him or he felt bad for her, but he instantly popped one hand out in front of her, indicating his agreement. She blushed, not intending him to do so. The old Will would have told her to get over herself. This Will, in a refined suit with gel in his hair, seemed gentle and eager to please.

Extending her hand as they do in the movies, she felt their fingertips touch and instantly started sweating. Why

The Purpose

she was nervous, she still didn't understand, but she felt unsure of how to move her feet and even more so, where she should look. If she looked in his eyes, it would deem a romantic moment. If she looked at the crowd, she would be caught staring intensely at Kyle. She settled on the ceiling as they started to move to the music. As her nerves finally retracted, she started to smile. She was having fun with Will and she was certain he felt the same. They danced to "Can You Feel The Love Tonight" by Elton John and she could almost feel herself floating. Kyle's eyes were locked on her, but she didn't even notice. Will smelled of his father's aftershave and his hands were strong and solid as he spun her into the crowd. Hearing his laugh, she leaned back as he dipped her and pulled her to him tightly around the waist. The song ended long before they separated and realized what had happened. She had never danced with Will before that night and she never did again.

Audrey caught herself smiling at the memory of her and Will when Mark sprung through the crowd with a beaming grin spreading from within his graying beard.

"My dear," he said, bowing before her.

"All right," she said, laughing. She couldn't help but love the big bear of man that he was. He scooped her up and twirled her around like she was seven years old again. Regardless of her aging year after year, he still danced with her like a little blonde girl in a dress full of toole and ribbons.

Almost the same height as him now, he barely looked down at her to utter the words everyone was avoiding.

The Purpose

"I know I am not supposed to talk about....what's his name," he said flatly.

Audrey sighed. If anyone would bring it up on a perfectly delightful spring afternoon, it would be Mark.

"It's okay," she mumbled, looking down at his shiny black shoes.

"Kid, I just love you, you know? I worry about you and it almost tore your sweet parents apart when they thought they'd lost you. I know it isn't my place, but dear Lord, I am so glad you are safe and sound back with the people that love you."

Audrey could feel tears brimming to the brink. She blinked hard and swallowed what felt like rocks in her throat. Mark reached for her chin and lifted it to meet him eye level. His pale blue eyes were overflowing with large, telling tears.

"I don't understand," he continued. "How could you let a man treat you that way? You of all people, my strong little Audrey bear. Oh, it drives me crazy, but I know I am out of line right now. I needed to tell you that we love you, that is all."

He hugged her tightly as they swayed back and forth to the rest of the song. She never met his gaze again throughout the rest of the party. She simply finished the dance and as he bowed again, she forced a thank you under her breath before heading back inside. She knew he was right and his intentions were sweet, but she wasn't ready to talk about it yet. She knew this party would be more about her coming back to her family, as opposed to her

The Purpose

graduation, but she was in disbelief that anyone would actually ask her about it. Even her father promised her, "If you come to the party, darlin', I won't speak a word of it, promise". Will had even remained silent, instead choosing to talk about his lack of approval of her career choice. Emma was an exception, and always would be. She knew everything there was and probably even more than Audrey knew sometimes. She had done her diligent duty of staging interesting stories and elaborate gestures to take the attention away from Audrey at the party, but big old Mark slipped through the cracks of her protection.

She was a new woman now; an educated, strong-willed Audrey and despite the plaguing sense of disappointment in herself, she would not let those remarks ruin a perfectly lovely affair. She spent the rest of party smiling through her frustration and being the daughter her parents pled of her until finally she excused herself as the sun set.

It wasn't until she slipped into the driver's side of her yellow Volkswagen Bug, set to be sold tomorrow, that she started to cry and didn't stop again until she reached her apartment. With the deepest of restraint, she resisted listening to her and Jason's song as the car lights blurred by her. It simply didn't matter how she wanted to feel; she had no control. She would always love him in the most desperate fashion.

Chapter 3

Mindless work was the most efficient way to forget her depression. Working in her glamorous position as a manager of no-kill animal shelter consistently offered refuge from the real world. Here she could wear work boots and blue jeans, her hair in a ponytail and little to no makeup. The only visitors were generally families with young children looking to adopt or middle-age divorcees on the brink of a mental breakdown if they didn't find their "new best friend". News flash, people, these sweet little babies will love you, but you have to love yourself first, she always thought. Often enough, depressed women would find themselves crying on her young bony shoulders, describing their loneliness in utter detail. For the last year or longer, Audrey had felt herself relating to them more than she cared to admit. Still, she found it the greatest pleasure to match the perfect shitzu to the widowed man or the most energetic tabby kitten to a playful four-year-old.

The Purpose

Her parents had been begging her to find a new career. "Cleaning cat boxes isn't real work, Audrey," her mother had scorned countless times. But Audrey loved it, despite their rude remarks and greedy expectations. Her pay came from donations and it consistently remained plenty to handle her bills and a little extra. She didn't need much, and although her father always tried to slip a hundred dollar bill into her purse during family dinners, she always retrieved it and left it on the table by the front door on her way out.

It was in this rescue center that Audrey found her own little piece of happiness three years ago by the name of August. August was a tiny black cat filled with enough energy to challenge even the most patient. Audrey had started volunteering at the shelter during her sophomore year of college, helping to sweep out cages, walk dogs and yes, change litter boxes. She had resisted taking any of the little angels home thus far, but as the days wore on and people consistently passed August by whispering, "He is bad luck because he is black," or "he looks sickly", there came a breaking point in her soul. She reached into a cage filled with other runny-nosed kittens and gently wiped the sleep from his eyes. His large-mouthed *meow* followed by a perfectly planned stretch made her laugh in spite of herself. "You're not bad luck; I don't care what they say," she whispered into his soft ears. Since that day, her little buddy was attached to her hip and no matter how many strings of bad luck she had been through; she refused to believe it was his fault.

He had seen her through many difficult moments,

including when Jason left. Although if he could talk, she is sure he would cry out in sheer joy at his leaving. She found herself spoiling him with an insane amount of catnip and treats after the one and *only* night he was abused. Jason and Audrey had been fighting; another reckless raging fight. Jason had thrown just about everything in the apartment as he screamed, "You worthless fat whore, you have no idea how lucky you are to be with me." She had crouched in the corner, as she often did, with her prized possessions flying overhead. She knew better than to reach out for them or try and stop him for fear of what he had done to her in the past. It was best just to let him go.

There was one possession he reached for that tore her heart to pieces instantly and forced her from her sheltered corner. It was as if she was in a horrendous nightmare and a fog of darkness overcame the room. Rage filled her, eyes shining black and sweat immediately forcing through her pores. She could only imagine how intensely psychotic she must have looked, but all be damned if she even remotely cared. She saw him reach for August, hold him high above his head and slam his innocent and fearful body onto his metal workout bench. August didn't even have time to hiss, meow or even understand what was happening. Suddenly his frail body was thrust with such force that she was utterly surprised his bones weren't shattered to pieces.

Before Jason could fully comprehend, Audrey was on his back, ripping, pulling and punching wherever her arms could reach.

"How dare you! He is innocent, you piece of shit!" she

The Purpose

screamed over her blows to his head, neck, stomach and finally his crotch. It was as if all of her pent up rage was finally released and he had no idea how to respond. She had always imagined this moment, the time when he went one too far, but she thought he would beat her senseless if she fought back. Here she was, beating the hell out of him and he stood in shock while she did so. He didn't move, didn't fight back, until finally she retreated to the other side of the room, her chest rising and falling.

It was then she realized the magnitude of what took place and fear rose from within. She started toward August when he lunged at her. Two inches from her face, he grabbed her by the hair and calmly said the words she would never forget.

"You will never be anyone. You are worthless and disgusting. The way your nose tilts up, your bulging stomach over your jeans, which by the way everyone thinks you're pregnant, but I would beat that baby out of you if it were true. You need to give up on life. Your family gave up on you a long time ago, and if it weren't for me, you'd be on the streets. Give up, Audrey, you ugly slut." And with the conclusion of his final gut-wrenching dig, he leaned back dramatically and spit in her face.

He was gone for three days and she later learned he was staying with a girl from work. Audrey spent hours crying, locked in her closet, rocking August back and forth, whispering how sorry she was. She packed her bags, called her sister and was ready to leave when he stormed through the door with flowers. He would never do it again, he

The Purpose

promised. He loved August, he loved her and their life. He claimed he had no idea how someone could be so stupid to mistreat her. He even fell to the floor and hugged her knees as *almost* believable tears dripped down her leg while she stood numb.

Emma had no idea truly what happened, but rather they had a fight. Had she known, the police would have been involved and Audrey ripped from her home. She didn't tell her because deep down in her heart, she was starting to believe she deserved it. She was afraid the words he repeated over and over again were true. No one would ever love her and she would never be anything. She wasn't smart. She had little to no talent, and turning to the side in the mirror, she could see why people would say she looked pregnant. When the pregnancy test revealed no, that in fact she was just putting on weight, she cried endlessly at the idea of him leaving her because she was no longer attractive.

This fight was the beginning of countless suicide notes, a complete disregard for eating and a decline in her relationship with everyone, even Emma. He was all she deserved and he knew it.

The animal shelter became her safe zone. Jason never knew where she worked, nor did he ever care. Since their final demise, she stayed in their mutual apartment for one month before she realized how dangerous it was. He would show up late at night, banging on her windows, shaking her soul to the core. He would key her car in long and hateful scratches, leave harassing messages on her phone and slip

The Purpose

hand-written notes in a criminal-like manner under her door. Several times he had been waiting by her car before work. Some days he would cry and beg her to take him back and others he would walk quickly behind her, whispering hateful names in her ear. Whether or not she knew where her strength came from, she had somehow found it and he had no idea how to handle it. After breaking down to Emma with the real truth, Emma drew a large breath, trying to calm herself before demanding she move to a new place.

Her new apartment was just blocks from the shelter and she walked to and from work despite the weather. Walks were her therapy and sense of solace, even during the winter months. She had sold her previous car, changed her cell phone number and removed all traces of herself from any mutual friends. Emma had been with her every step of the way and Audrey complied like she belonged with the witness protection program. No matter the distance between her and the old version of herself, she still felt lost and afraid. Even worse, she still found herself missing the good times. She would catch herself thinking of the way he laughed at himself when telling a story. She still slept in his old t-shirt left behind and cried herself to sleep, dreaming of the days she felt happy.

Emma constantly reminded her how beautiful she was and that she deserved the moon and the stars. She bought her countless books on "battered-women's syndrome" and assured her that this is exactly how *he* wanted her to feel. She read a chapter or two before declaring disturbing similarities and slamming the book shut. She would deal

The Purpose

with her life and the horrible memories on her own time. For the time being, she chose to frantically erase over her written story like a kindergartener with a large, square pink eraser.

"Can I hold the little beagle?" a small voice piped into Audrey's train of thought.

"Huh? Oh, sure. Let me grab a key." She led the small girl with bright red hair to FIL room.

Audrey came back with the small beagle puppy that whined with every step.

"What does F. I. L mean," the little girl stuttered.

"It means our *Fall In Love* room," said Audrey with a smile.

"This little lady is extremely special. She was found on the side of the road five weeks ago. Her eyes weren't even open and we had to bottle feed her," Audrey said softly.

The little girl's eyes widened with fear. "Is she okay now?"

"Well, we had to do a little surgery because her back leg was broken, but with extra love and care, she is almost back to normal. She will be just fine," she said and smiled.

Audrey gently placed the shaking puppy into the little girl's hands and showed her how to soothe her nerves with long strokes along her back. In no time, she was nestled against her stomach, her eyes starting to close.

Audrey stepped back as the little girl spoke softly to the puppy. "I will love you forever and ever."

A moment later, a tap on the glass door behind her jostled her nerves. Audrey spun around to see an equally small little boy with the same red hair and a matching father. Cracking the door, she ushered them in and introduced herself. The family gathered around the little beagle as the little girl told them her story.

Audrey wrapped her arms around herself. This was the reason she did this, because of moments like this. This little beagle was going to be just fine.

"Well, sweetheart, what will you name her?" the father asked, winking at Audrey.

"Oh, Daddy, can we keep her? I want to name her Grace," she said and beamed.

"Why Grace?" asked Audrey, always curious to know the meaning behind the name.

"Because God's grace is the reason she is alive," the little girl noted proudly.

Audrey's breath caught at the sound of such a profound statement from a seemingly seven or eight-year-old girl. Her father watched over her with pride, but barely flinched. This must be a common occurrence of intelligence from her.

"Absolutely right," Audrey said, squatting down to meet her eye level. "And His grace is the same reason she found you."

As the sweet red-headed family left with Grace the beagle, Audrey excused herself to the bathroom. With the door quietly shut behind her, she felt tears drip down her face as she thanked God for beauty within even the darkest hours.

Her walk home that evening was filled with lighter memories of her childhood. She consciously forced herself

The Purpose

to think on a more positive note, as even her own depression was becoming too much for her. The spring air floated through her curls and the sunlight played behind the clouds. She tiptoed from the sidewalk to the street, with each step humming a tune. Could she be releasing her sadness or did she simply have a good day? It was too early to tell and she didn't even want to think about it right now. Her thoughts drifted to the night her father took her horse back riding as a surprise present for her perfect report card.

"Don't you think my girl deserves a sweet reward for a job well done?" he said and chuckled with great pride.

The stars were out on a warm summer's eve in Missouri, but more importantly the moon was in full blast splashing across the field of her grandpa's farm. It was just the two of them; Emma's surprise was to come later. She stood right by his side as he gently placed the saddle on the white mare, Shae, before hoisting Audrey up on her back. Audrey reached for Shae's marshmallow colored hair and lightly braided it before her father gave her the cue to take off.

"Let's ride!" he bellowed into the night. She found her place next to him and his horse, Beans. They rode in silence while the black sky stretched around them and the warm breeze tickled her arms and legs. Shae didn't need much instruction, perhaps the reason Audrey's dad had chosen her, but nevertheless Audrey felt strong and in control. They talked softly as if telling secrets after slowing the horses to a walk.

"What do you dream about, darlin'?" her dad asked.

The Purpose

"Oh, Dad, don't be silly." She felt herself flush.

"Now, Audrey bear, that is as serious a question as the day is long. You should always be dreaming about something, and even more so, trying to make those dreams a reality," he said. "Just 'cause you're nine years old don't mean nothing. Your dreams still count."

"Well okay, then," she mumbled. She sat up straighter and pushed her feet further into the stirrups. "I suppose I dream about what kind of a woman I'm gonna be."

"Is that so? Well, what do you think, my dear?"

"I don't think I am gonna be like Mom. Not in a bad way, you know? Just that I think I will be a little stronger. I really want to do something big, like be a country singer, travel the world or write books. Mom doesn't seem to have many dreams." She trailed off.

"Now wait just one minute, sweetheart. Your mama has many dreams, but her most prized dream is you and Emma. She has lived a beautiful life and chose every minute of it. All that we wish for you is to do the same; fulfill the dreams you are chasing."

Audrey settled into her saddle and thought about her father's words. How do you choose your life? How do you even know where to begin? Her father hummed along as he sped up to a trot and Audrey followed suit. She heard his loud laughter split through the night as Beans lifted from the ground and let out an equally loud *neigh*.

That night is permanently inscribed in her story to this very day. Some memories may haunt you endlessly, but some pop out of the blue at precisely the right time to keep

The Purpose

you putting one foot in front of the other. Graduation had come and gone, and Audrey was ready to start anew. The question remained; what exactly would that lead her to find?

* * * *

"No excuses, not tonight," said Emma in an accusatory tone.

"Well, I…fine. What time?" asked Audrey.

"Six o'clock, so don't be late. We are attempting to make a something soy for you and plenty of fresh greens."

"You shouldn't have," she attempted, but Emma had already hung up the phone. Her sister was so persistent. Peering at the clock, she realized it was already five and she had yet to do any laundry or shower after her long exhausting day. She padded to the kitchen, ripped open six boxes to finally find her nicer clothes wrinkled and rammed into the bottom of the last one. "Nice," she mumbled before ripping open another box to look for the iron. Normally she wouldn't dress up for dinner at her sister's house, but tonight was the celebration dinner for Alex's new firm. He had finally spread his wings and was attempting to build his own clientele with a friend of his that also practiced family law. Emma was bringing out the nice china and serving champagne with dinner, so Audrey assumed her rubber work boots and muddy jeans wouldn't make the cut.

Her apartment was still in shambles and she found little to no energy to unpack anything she wasn't in dire need of. The two-bedroom actually boasted intricate features that could eventually make for a beautiful home. Crown molding

The Purpose

lined the walls. Dark wooden floors that creaked slightly with every other step and periodic stone-cracked pillars on either side of arched entryways helped fill the 1920s townhouse style apartment building with character. There was a grand bay window overlooking a garden filled with rose bushes, lilacs and tulips that were overgrown and seemed to be alive with each wind that passed. Although the appliances were outdated and the bathroom tub literally had claw feet on it, Audrey couldn't pass it by. It was her home; it spoke to her and she refused to be convinced that she needed granite counter tops and stainless steel.

The landlord probably sold her on the new home more than anything. A lively woman in her seventies named Claudia lived below her in the only other apartment in the building. She had silver hair mixed with streaks of black that was always wrapped in a loose bun held together with what looked like yarn braided in various colors. Fake eyelashes and deep red blush and lipstick lit her face up. She always dressed in her finest: long ball gowns either too big or small and most likely bought from the local thrift store.

Her home was filled with portraits of all of the people she had known in her seventy years, or rather as she called them, her teachers. They were stacked up and down the walls, some with serious and unnerving expressions and others filled with glee. She constantly had paint in various colors splashed on her cheeks, forehead and arms. Claudia had an English accent that Audrey couldn't help but wonder if it was real.

"Darling," she extended out a long overly-dramatic

The Purpose

breath, "won't you please stay here in my little castle? This will be where you dreams come alive and at last your true self shall be uncovered!"

Audrey had signed on the line despite Emma's better judgment, but who could resist an imposter English woman that insisted upon her friendship. Who was she to deny any friend at this point, even is she was off her rocker?

Fresh out of the shower, she heard her door bell ring. It was the first time it had rung since moving in and it echoed like a grandfather clock across the bare walls and floors, sending a shiver down Audrey's spine.

Sliding on her yellow spring dress covered in white daisies, she raced to the door, hair still dripping wet. Claudia stood, elegant as ever in a metallic maroon dress with golden lace. "Hello Audrina," she whispered as she pushed past her into the apartment. "Lovely dress, although your hair needs a bit of work."

"Uh thanks, I just got out of the shower."

"That is precisely why I am here to see you, darling."

"Oh?"

"Yes, you see, I am having a gathering of some sorts. A Ball, if you will, and I would be deeply disturbed if you didn't attend."

"A Ball?" Audrey repeated.

"Yes, downstairs this Friday. Dress appropriately; none of those little girl clothes. Let me know if you need to borrow."

With that, Claudia whisked away, leaving only the concerned look on Audrey's face. This woman seriously

The Purpose

was missing in the mental department. She could see it now, Audrey and Claudia standing in her apartment, music floating from the record player, only the two of them to drink the aged wine and no one to dance with at the Ball. Audrey giggled before closing her door and marking *Claudia's Ball* in red marker on her calendar hanging in the kitchen; remarkably the only thing unpacked. Ironically, there were simply three or four other events in the month's time, which was hardly worth a calendar at all.

Slipping on her silver ballet flats, she gave August a kiss goodbye and headed out the door to make the seven and a half minute ride to Emma's house.

* * * *

"Will's here!" screeched Emma, pulling her into the house before she could even set her purse down.

"Why on earth? We never see him and now twice in a month?"

"Mom and Dad invited Mark and I guess he just tagged along for the ride. Don't be rude, he is still like family."

"Sure, family you never see but every five years."

Heading for the kitchen, she heard Mark's boisterous laugh and her mother's voice talking excitedly about some sort of trip.

"What's going on?" Emma asked, rounding the corner.

"My dear!" Audrey's father, mother and Mark all lunged for her at the same time. One after one they smothered her in hugs and kisses before getting back to Emma's question. Will nodded at her as if to say hello from across the room where he stood leaning against the counter top.

"We were talking about Will," Mark started. "He is heading to Norwich, England, to study abroad at the Norfolk & Norwich University Hospital in the summer."

"Wow, really?" Emma said. "Congratulations, Will, we are so proud of you."

Audrey stood bemused as Will smiled with gratitude.

"How long?" Emma continued.

"He will be there for six months to a year, depending on the amount of work to be completed within the program," Mark answered.

Audrey's silence continued, in shock. How on earth had Will become so accomplished as she stood idly by with life swarming around her? It unnerved her to envision him making his way through the world, while she played dress up with her crazy neighbor on Friday nights. She knew she should be happy for him, but truthfully, jealousy was the only immediate emotion she could conjure. The doorbell broke her concentration and she excused herself from the room and her own thoughts.

Standing with perfect posture and a new suit, Blake looked nervous. He reached forward with his bottle of wine and took a deep breath before saying, "You must be Audrey." Instantly, Audrey new this was a set-up. If she knew Emma at all, this had to be one of her master plans. She had to admit, she did good. He was classic handsome with deep set green eyes and sandy blond hair and the most perfectly white, straight teeth she had ever seen. Immediately entranced, she leaned forward for the wine and tripped over the burgundy rug tucked in the entrance way.

"You must be Blake," she said and grinned back. "Emma and Alex have told me quite a bit about you. Congrats, by the way."

"All good things I hope," he said and winked.

Oh lord, she was in trouble. The last thing she needed, and Emma knew it, was to fall into the hands of an eighty hour a week working lawyer who categorized her as another notch on his belt. She was dealing with some serious issues, trying to rebound back to a regular routine and find what little confidence she had left. She immediately made a conscious decision to resist his charm and intoxicating good looks. She took his coat, trying to deny the instant ominous feel from her heart.

"So, Audrey," Blake cleared his throat, "Alex says you are working for a nonprofit?"

"Foreign concept to you," she muttered.

"Huh?"

"Um, yeah. Animal shelter," she answered flatly. Walking briskly to the kitchen to avoid any further conversation, she was met with a sneaky glance from Emma.

"Everyone, this is Alex's new partner!" Emma beamed. "He attended Stanford Law and recently moved back home to St. Louis to be closer to his family."

Emma rambled as if selling him on eBay, highlighting his most charming characteristics. Mid-sentence, Audrey tuned out, focusing instead on the expression on her father's face. He seemed concerned, puzzled.

The Purpose

"Dad?" She leaned her head against him.

"Yes, bear? What's on your mind?"

"You worried about something? You seem like you are miles away from this kitchen."

"Nothin' you need to concern yourself with," he said and nodded. "Here, have some sweet plum wine. Your mother says it warms the soul, but I do believe she means it makes her menopause kick in." He chuckled.

He never knew how to be honest with her. Ever since she was a little girl, she could see his every expression poured out upon his face. It was impossible for him to keep a secret, and if it killed her, she planned on getting an answer tonight.

Dinner consisted of chicken parmesan, soy for Audrey, and sweet roasted red pepper pasta sprinkled with grated cheese. Her mom was right and the plum wine rolled down her throat and nestled into the pit of her stomach, swirling enough to make her feel peaceful. She could feel her cheeks getting rosy and only realized she had a bit too much when she reached for the biscuits and knocked her glass over sideways. Frantically searching for a towel or napkin, she was met with a calming smile by Blake wiping wine from her placemat, her arm and finally her cheek. If wine splashed on her cheek from across the table, there was surely a misunderstanding. She sat perfectly still as he swept around her, cologne invading her space. Emma smiled all the while with an approving glance. There must have been a serious "set-up" conversation between the two of them prior to this evening. They interacted with such unspoken

The Purpose

awareness that it literally made Audrey sick to her stomach.

Excusing herself, she headed for the kitchen only to run into Will; awe-inspiring, ambitious Will. He continued opening every drawer, pretending to ignore her.

"Now who doesn't have the answers?" she prodded. This suburban house was starting to suffocate her and this conversation would more than likely do her in. Each drawer slammed after the next, forcing silverware to dance around inside. Will adjusted his tie, ran his hands over his facial scruff and backed away from the counter.

"What is your deal?" he mumbled, looking her up and down. "I haven't seen you at all in like five years and here you are acting like the brat you have always been. Can't we have a nice dinner here or are you better suited getting drunk on cheap wine and tearing your sister's highly anticipated evening to a pre-meditated torture fest. Get over yourself." His eyes settled on the metal pie server to the left of the stove. Reaching for it, he grazed her hip and rested his eyes upon her face. "You're not the only one with problems," he said. His hot breath pressed into her.

Damn him.

After dessert, the family nestled in around the fireplace. Blake smiled intensely at Audrey as she told stories of recent adoptions, while Will glared from across the room. When the laughter died down, Blake reached for her hand.

"Do you have a favorite composer?" He searched her blank expression.

"Blake is a gifted pianist," announced Emma from across the room with once again planned flattery.

The Purpose

Stretching and popping his long delicate fingers, Blake smoothed his pleated pants and poised gingerly on the edge of the piano bench. Anticipation filled the room as he rattled off the composer and the name of the piece, something with "choskey" on the end of it. Softly, the music began to build and the room became enveloped with a Broadway performance. In an unreal state, this beautiful man scaled the keyboard with such intensity that Audrey felt something leap inside her. Intense or not, there was something different about this one. For what felt like only seconds, the heart-wrenching notes tore apart her inhibitions and left her wounded at his appeal. The applause erupted around her as he spun around, offering a wink in her direction. *Whatever.*

"I could teach you, you know?"

Audrey glanced sideways to meet Blake's question as he walked her to her cab. The wind picked up, ushering a brisk chill flooding up her sleeves and at her bare legs. The weatherman may claim it is spring, but the chilly nights begged to differ.

"Teach me what?" she asked, wishing she hadn't.

"The piano," he said and grinned. "I would love to share it with you. You truly have the perfect fingers," he whispered, reaching for her hand and caressing her fingers with the world's most gentle touch.

She heard herself echo a soft, "I would like that."

Chapter 4

Unsure of what bothered her more, the impulsive attraction for Blake, or the irritating run-in with Will, Audrey stretched her legs against the curb outside of her townhouse. Running would be her newest love affair and she had read precisely three magazine articles instructing her how to hit the ground running. Her walks soothed her soul, but jogging would whittle her middle. Reaching for the sky, one arm outstretched above the other, she felt her anxiety begin to loosen. *Nothing to it*, she thought, before starting at a slow stride. Instantly, her legs began to burn and her thighs tightened. The blood rushed to her chest and her breathing escaped. This is not what the magazine said would happen. She was supposed to feel "enriched with the quickening pace" and "succumb to the right of the race". She forced herself to keep going, spotting a stop sign about a hundred yards away as her goal.

The Purpose

Panting like a puppy dog after a chew toy, she hugged the sign's pole with an unyielding grip. Cars zoomed past her with little regard to her near death experience as she stood gasping for air. How was this possibly enjoyable for anyone? A coffee shop at the corner pulled her across traffic and she settled in for a sweet caramel macchiato. She could walk around the neighborhood a bit, and maybe look into yoga. For now, sweet bliss tickled her nose and the warm buzz of commotion of businessmen and chatty stay-at-home moms with babies in tow was enough of a distraction. The warm hint of cinnamon played at her senses when suddenly her phone came bursting to life. The crowd seemed to silence as everyone stared at her frantically searching through her jacket on the back of her chair.

"Hello?" She almost dropped the phone. The coffee shop crowd roared to life again.

"Audrey? This is Blake. Hope I am not catching you at a bad time."

Oh geez, was this guy serious? How on earth....Emma! Surely she gave him her number.

"Oh no problem, just out for a jog. What's up?"

"Good for you! I love a good run in the morning. Well, your sister passed along your number because to be honest, well, I haven't stopped thinking about you."

Gosh, he was so cliché. Did men really say those things anymore? Yet somehow, it was hardly inappropriate for him.

"That's sweet. I had a nice time, too."

"So, you interested in dinner sometime? Maybe Friday night?"

The Purpose

"Um, well you should know..."

"Look, Emma gave me the background. Truly, I am not out to make your life more complicated. I felt a connection with you, something rare, and I really wanted to see if there was anything to it. No games, promise."

"I guess. Emma will kill me if I don't." *Was that out loud?*

"I'll take it! Even if it is a pity date. How about I meet you at Malian's at eight on Friday?"

"See you then." She hung up the phone with instant regret. She wasn't ready and she knew it. Emma could be such an intrusive pain, but after all, she said yes. No one was there to twist her arm, and who could forget those fierce green eyes. Six months after Jason, and she finally entered the *Dating Someone Else* phase.

* * * *

Friday sprung on her so quickly, it seemed unreal. Sheer panic and fear flooded through her all morning at work and well into the evening. Staring out into the garden she pictured herself elegantly strolling toward Blake. She planned on wearing her two-inch heels because his height could afford it. She'd even bought a new dress for the occasion, a black satin strapless. Emma insisted it was the sexiest thing she had ever seen on her, and Audrey couldn't help but agree. The dress screamed "take me in your arms" even if her heart didn't.

She had waxed every inch of herself and curled, then straightened her hair. The nerves were getting to the point of

The Purpose

exhaustion, so before heading out the door, she slammed a one hitter of cherry vodka. A little drunk, a little giddy, she walked the four blocks uphill in heels to her Italian destiny.

* * * *

The melodic sound of the doorbell rang in her ears as the hostess greeted her immediately. About sixteen years of age, too much eyeliner and almond-colored hair in an up do that appeared to have taken at least an hour offered her a sympathetic smile.

"You must be Audrey," she said matter-of-factly.

"Yes, actually, I am meeting someone here."

"Blake? Yes, he said you would be here at eight."

"Well, okay. Has he arrived?"

"He has, but not here. He wanted me to give you this." She reached behind the hostess stand and gently retrieved a dark golden envelope with "Audrey" inscribed in a script impression. Looking from the envelope to the adult-looking hostess, she felt her stomach sink.

"He is standing me up? Are you freaking kidding me? I knew it! This is the first time I have been on a date since my jackass of an ex, and I truly thought this guy was different. I give up, I swear!" Audrey handed the envelope back and proceeded to head toward the door.

"Um, Audrey," the waitress called out. "I don't think that is what this envelope was going to tell you. Don't you think you should read it first?"

Audrey spun around, embarrassment undeniably spreading across her flushed cheeks.

The Purpose

"Just kidding." She laughed, grabbed the envelope and headed out the door.

Walking slowly down the sidewalk, light rain tickled her eyelashes. She took a deep breath and slid her pointer finger along the golden envelope opening. The card was plain white on the front, with a tiny image of a golden horse in the bottom right corner. Its mane was floating in an imaginary wind and it seemed to be smiling at her. Flipping open the card, she was greeted with the same scripture handwriting that read, *"Meet me in Forest Park ~Love, Blake (P.S. Don't worry, your family knows where you are ☺)"*.

Stunned, she read and re-read the two sentences. Closing the card, she looked up to hail a cab, only to see a shiny black town car waiting in front of her.

"Miss Audrey Landrow," a gentleman in a black suit spoke out.

"Yes?"

"Mr. Maddox is expecting you in Forest Park on this fine evening. May I offer you a lift?"

Either she was about to be listed on the evening news as an unsuspecting murder victim or this had to be the most romantic man she had ever encountered.

"Can you just give me one second?" she said and smiled sweetly to the driver.

"Of course, Miss Landrow. Take your time."

Dialing Emma, as she was sure Blake expected her to do; she wasn't at all surprised to hear her overly eager voice on the other end of the call.

The Purpose

"Are you so excited?" Emma screamed into the phone.

"Actually, I am. How much do you know?"

"Oh no, you are not getting details out of me. Just know that you need to get into that beautiful town car sitting in front of you and head to Forest Park. I know exactly where you will be, so no danger, I promise. Although, I probably should have had you wear a different outfit. Okay, 'bye!" With one fluent, exasperated statement, Emma hung up the phone, leaving Audrey speechless.

A wide grin stretching across her unsuspecting face made her squeal in delight. Brushing the glisten of tiny silver droplets of rain from her cheeks, she nodded to the driver and slipped inside the smooth sedan.

* * * *

There he stood, every ounce of his sensitive manliness bundled into the perfect combination of what she was never looking for. How could this be? How on earth did he steal her heart within two encounters? Under a large oak tree stretching across the starlet spring evening sky, he was holding out a large present with a glittery bow. He was dressed in a loose version of business-casual with a white polo shirt tucked under a mint green sweater vest and khakis. She blinked twice at the thought of dreaming, only to open to the same perfect image. He was real, and her sister could attest to his genuineness.

"Hey, gorgeous." He smiled, effortlessly beautiful.

"I don't know what to say. This is unreal, like a dream." She reached to pull her strapless dress up a bit around her bust line and straightened her skirt. Luckily, the rain had stopped with little damage to the ground and her heels stood firmly against the grass. He set the present on the ground temporarily to reach and pull her into a tight embrace. He smelled of smoked chestnuts and aftershave. Audrey felt her stomach leap again, which was ridiculous.

Pulling away from her, he flashed those perfectly white teeth and said, "Now, open your gift!"

She untwisted the bow made of satin and glitter, peeled back the paper and landed her eyes on a large shoe box. Clearly this box only held her real gift. She glanced up at Blake questionably. He started laughing, but gestured for her to continue. Inside the box were two, sandy brown, leather riding boots tucked in golden paper.

"They are fake leather, because you don't eat meat. Hope that is okay." Blake gently reached within the box to pull them out on display. "You see, a little bird told me just how much you used to love horseback riding."

Just then, two gleaming thoroughbred horses caught the corner of her eye. They were led by a trainer dressed to the nines in old-fashioned jockey attire. Guiding them by their lead rope tucked under their chins, he seemed so tiny. They were the tallest and most glamorous horses she had ever seen, easily seventeen hands tall; one solid midnight black with silky matching mane, the other light brown with blond hair and eyelashes. Her breath caught in her throat and tears brimmed over her eyes. This was the most magical she had felt in years, straight from a fairytale.

"I can't believe...I am..." she stuttered.

The Purpose

"Don't say a word. If anyone deserves this it is you."

Reaching one timid hand forward, she felt the coarse hair run through her fingers. She smiled and cupped her hand under the black horse's nose for him to smell her. He nuzzled her hand and snorted loudly. The eyelashes are the most beautiful part of any horse and peering out from under his were coal-colored marbles. He seemed smart, a horse far beyond his years, like he sensed her emotion. She wanted nothing more than to put on those riding boots and ride off into the wind, but suddenly she felt faint and lightheaded. She leaned back away from the horses to try and steady herself. One large breath, then another; air couldn't come fast enough. Blake reached for her, but it was too late. She fell, far from gracefully, to the ground with her eyes closed tightly. Her dress had slid up around her stomach, allowing her pink panties with the word "Purrfect" written on them to be on full display.

* * * *

Blinking repeatedly, Audrey tried to focus. What was that obnoxious beeping sound and who in God's name was talking so loudly?

"Don't you think we should still take her?"

She knew that voice. It reminded her of a friend she used to know.

"Yes, sir. I do believe it is her best interest to get a full examination. If nothing else, to ease everyone's mind. It was probably a lack of eating properly, low blood sugar, something of that nature."

The Purpose

Okay, that voice she didn't know. Reaching for the handles on the ambulance stretcher, (*ambulance stretcher?*), she pulled herself up and everyone started talking even louder.

Blake was the first to lunge at her, smoothing her hair out of her face and talking extremely fast. He was a fuzzy blur and she only caught every third word. She had passed out right under the horse's feet on their first date. *Fantastic.*

"I am okay, really." She started to get up. "I am just gonna go home. Blake, can you give me a ride?"

"Sorry, ma'am," said the tall man in the uniform in a firm voice. We need to take you in as a protocol. If everything checks out all right, you will be home resting in no time. Is this by chance a recurring act of yours?" The EMS worker was obviously near retirement and irritated as all hell to be answering calls of girls passing out in the park. He was scribbling frantically on a notepad stuck to a clipboard, his walkie talkie continuing to sound off emergencies.

"No, sir." She felt ashamed, embarrassed and if possible, so very alone. Blake was sweet and tentative, but she wanted someone familiar she could wrap her arms around, someone who could hold her tightly, all the while laughing hysterically at the situation.

With a loud grunt, which was oddly unsettling, the two EMS men hoisted her, stretcher and all, up into the ambulance. Blake held her hand, whispering reassuring and soothing gestures until the last possible second. The doors slammed behind her leaving Forest Park, her dream horses and the perfect spring evening only to her imagination.

The Purpose

* * * *

After what seemed like twenty-four hours of paperwork, several calls from her family and a ghastly amount of nurses and doctors prodding at her, she was finally left alone to rest while they analyzed the tests. Freezing cold in her nightgown with strings that refused to hold the backside closed, she huddled under the covers, wishing she were home. Blake had insisted on staying, even though she refused to let him sit in the room with her. She knew it was a selfish move, but she had caught a glimpse of herself in the metal cabinet doors and there was no way this night was going to be savored in his memory with her looking like that. There is only so much a girl can do with no makeup to undo the damage of passing out. They had stuffed crackers and juice down her throat like she was a child and she currently had an IV lodged inside her most sensitive vein. How people are strong enough to battle cancer or any sort of serious disease amazed her. This is the only thing she could think of. Poor children, aging seniors or even women with breast cancer flooded her mind, forcing her to picture the most gruesome situations. Hospitals were filled with comforting pictures, sweet smelling coffee stations and inspiring chapels, but the truth remained that they were still filled with sickness and sadness. Her mind wrestled with how she might volunteer here in the future; now that she had spent her only real adequate amount of time in one, there was surely an opportunity she was missing. Maybe this was a sign. Possibly the OB or even the emergency room would be the best place for her.

The Purpose

"Hey, kid," a voice from behind the curtain called out. "Can I come in?"

Kid? That wasn't the doctor's voice that said he would be right back.

"Um, who is it?" Her voice came out a weak, childlike cry.

"Will," the voice answered back.

"My Will? Will Michaels?"

"Yours truly." He laughed. "Can I come in or what?"

"Yeah, what are you doing here? How did you find me?"

Her questioned was answered as he flung the curtain aside and slipped inside her little world. He was dressed in blue scrubs with a surgical mask hanging around his neck.

"Oh," she said and sighed, "I forgot you were doing your residency here. What happened to HIPPA and patient confidentiality?"

"Your mom doesn't exactly comply with those policies," he mumbled, reading the monitor next to her bedside and then reaching to examine her IV bag. He plopped into the chair next to her and lifted the surgical mask from around his neck and flipped it back and forth within his hands.

"Saw your boyfriend in the waiting area," he said and grinned. "Either you got yourself a husband or you have screwed this guy up royally."

"What is that supposed to mean? Like I planned this? Look, Will, I am not in the mood for your…"

"Calm down, kid. I am here to take your mind off the

The Purpose

situation; just trying to make you laugh a bit."

"Nice job," she hissed and leaned back to close her eyes on the small, firm pillow.

"Let's try again. Why don't you tell me what happened?"

"I don't remember much of anything. All I remember is seeing the beautiful horses walking toward me and then *Bam! Ta da!*" For the first time, real laughter came spilling out as she realized how pathetically funny the story was. "I mean, would you ever call me again if I put you through this and didn't even let you wait in here with me?"

Will shrugged his shoulders and slid his tennis shoes onto the side of the bed. "To be honest, it is kind of cute." Instead of looking nervous and awkward, he seemed calm and relaxed. "I mean, you have that whole dorky thing going on." *There it is.*

"I knew you couldn't be nice. After all, I never see you dating anyone, now do I? Then again, you are never even around."

"Don't go getting testy with me; I work like ninety hours a week. I usually sleep here or should sleep here. Besides, you were entirely too busy with what's his name to know where any of your family was."

"Not fair, you don't know the half of it." She looked as if she might cry.

"Then tell me; tell someone. You can't pretend it never happened."

"I am not really in the mood, and if I were, it wouldn't be you that I told."

The Purpose

"Fair enough," he grunted before flipping the curtain open and walking out.

Left alone once more, silent tears started to roll down her whitened cheeks. Why couldn't he just be a friend? Why did he always have to say harsh, judgmental things that ripped her apart?

* * * *

Another hour longer and Dr. Tandasky returned with the results of her testing. She was diagnosed as passing out from extreme emotional distress and a tinge of anemia. The lack of red blood cells circulating in her system resulted in a sense of dizziness and shortness of breath. He prescribed an iron supplement and told her to get plenty of rest, assuring her the rest of her tests were fine.

Blake was right there waiting when she came walking out. He looked utterly exhausted with dark bags hanging below each of his eyes. After all, it was only three in the morning and she could only imagine his workload forced him to work an enormous amount of hours this week. His hair was ruffled, shirt un-tucked, but smile ever present.

"Hey, gorgeous." His grin spread from ear to ear.

"Oh God, please. I am so sorry, Blake."

He reached for her and held her in his arms for a long time without saying a single word. They swayed back and forth and she felt herself give in to him. Finally, the hug she had been longing for.

Chapter 5

A large pounding woke Audrey from the deepest of sleeps around noon the next morning. She wrestled with her blankets, rolled her eyes at herself in the mirror and flung open the front door. There stood Claudia in all her grandeur with yellow, orange and sage green paint smeared on various parts of her face and hands. Her false eyelashes were squinting at her and she tapped her finger impatiently against the door frame. From first impression, she was every bit of angry.

Before Audrey could speak, she belted out, English accent and all, "How could you?"

"What? What did I do?" Audrey was stunned and off put.

"Oh nothing, only my Ball." Claudia's eyes grazed the floor and the emotion drained from her face. "Darling, it simply wasn't the same without you."

The Purpose

"Oh my God, I completely forgot. I feel terrible. Let me make it up to you; do you have plans today?"

"Well, what do you have in mind? I suppose I could rearrange my schedule."

"I have the worst story to tell you; you'll never believe it. Come on in and we will figure something equally as exciting to do." She reached for the door, but Claudia slid her hand against the dark wood panel and said, "My dear, get dressed and come downstairs. I have some things to show you." With that, she was gone, only her perfume left as a reminder.

An hour later, Audrey sat twirling her blonde tendril, entranced around several photograph albums, Frank Sinatra singing elegantly in the background. Claudia flipped from picture to picture, each with yellowed edges showing their age. She had lived an extraordinary life and Audrey never would have guessed. There she stood, glamorous and Hollywood-like beautiful with countless different men. She was dancing, singing at a piano bar, swimming in the ocean, posing under the Eifel Tower and skiing down the slopes of the Rockies. She had always been tall and incredibly thin with long, flowing black-as-night hair. Her outfits were so normal and expensive looking, only the most elegant furs, pearls and party dresses. Audrey glanced from Claudia back to the pictures and tried to hide her puzzled expression.

The next page revealed a stack of brittle paper tucked inside the album. Each piece was worn and smudged, but the scribbled writing could still be read. "Dear Claudia," started each letter and as she began to read through the first page, Claudia snatched them from her hands.

"Now those are not for you to read. There are too many memories in there to start hashing through. I haven't got the energy today."

"You won't even tell me who they are from?" Audrey questioned.

"No, dear, not today. Maybe another time. Oh look, here I am with my mother." Claudia tapped the photo album with a long bony finger polished in eggplant purple. "I must have only been about twenty-three there and that is when she was starting to get sick. She was so careful with my feelings, always encouraging me to get out there and see the world. She came down with yellow fever that year, and it became more serious, causing hemorrhaging in her liver until she finally died. We spent every day that summer walking in the garden and I listened intently as she told me of her dreams." Claudia closed her eyes and a single tear fell onto her forest green-colored dress. "You see, dear, she always wanted to live a real life. A life with purpose, you know?"

"Didn't she consider you her purpose?"

"No, sweet child, sometimes a woman needs more. They have to dig deep to figure it out, figure out what makes their hearts leap. It isn't always a family or even a man. More often than not, it is the deepest of passions that a woman has yet to pursue. Something you just have to get out of your system before you die. Something God gave to you to love and cherish." With the last sentence, her accent slipped slightly and her breath shuddered as she spoke.

The Purpose

"What is your purpose, Claudia?"

"Oh, darling, mine has always been painting. The brush is an extension of my soul and pours my most inner thoughts onto the canvas. I used to travel the world you know, showing my art in various displays. People used to pay a great deal of money for my work and that was my ticket out. Along the way in all of my travels, I fell in love a hundred different times, but there was never anything that gave me peace like painting did."

As she spoke, Audrey scanned the walls to see her paintings through a new set of eyes. The portraits were made of a rainbow of colors in softened brushstrokes. Each person's expression was irresistible and so natural. Some were laughing with eyes squinted and their heads thrown back. You could almost hear their deep-rooted laughter, while others looked solemn and alone. How might Claudia paint her, she wondered? Would she forever embed her on canvass with a joyful expression, or would she capture her in a saddened state? Initially, she had seen Claudia's room full of faces as disturbing, but now she saw the memories they held.

Claudia caught her glance and followed her eyes to a very small portrait of a man with gleaming blue eyes. His hair was slicked to one side and his smile consumed most of his face. He was happy and filled with life and there was something oddly familiar about him.

"What is his name?" She extended her arm to point at the painting tucked in the corner of the room next to window.

"Well, I guess you would have found out eventually."

The Purpose

Claudia threw her head back with laughter. "A girl can't keep secrets from her friends."

She walked with ease toward the tiny portrait, wrapped her hands around it and took a deep breath. She brought it over and held it out to Audrey with straightened arms.

"I am sure he does look familiar to you. That is because he is the one singing on this record. We had the sweet affair for four whole months when I had just turned twenty-one years of age. Frank was a remarkable part of my life during that time, but his depression became too much for me to handle."

"I'm sorry....you had an affair with Frank Sinatra?" Audrey gasped.

"Oh, darling, it really isn't that fascinating. We met at a party in Los Angeles and dated for a bit. Frank was a very lost man during that time and much too old for me. He had just divorced his second wife, Ava. Their love affair was tumultuous and torturous." She shuddered at the memory.

"What happened?"

"With Ava? Oh, she was a viper of sorts, always running around on him. She was the only woman Frank could never tame. I think he saw me as a sweet, innocent woman he could love without complications. Over those few months, even though he was basically twice my age, I realized I deserved better."

"You turned down Frank Sinatra?" Audrey's mouth hung open.

"Well, I wouldn't put it that way. I had the opportunity to show some of my art in England, so it was the perfect

The Purpose

getaway. I left his mansion in Palm Springs with a swift kiss on his cheek and told him I would call him in a month. I do believe we both knew that would never happen. We never even spoke again. Call it turning down Frank, I wouldn't dream. Sometimes a woman has to take matters into her own hands and slip quietly out the back door. A ruckus is often more trouble than it is worth. He went on to marry again and I do believe he was quite happy with that last one."

"Wow," was all Audrey could muster.

"Ha! You are too much, girl." Claudia smiled. "Don't you worry; you will have your chance. Remember, I told you your true self would be discovered here? There is something about this place that awakens the soul. It was my parents' home at one point and I found myself unable to let it go to waste. She still lives within these walls; I can feel her."

Audrey glanced toward the window with the sun beaming in. At long last, she discovered Claudia's history and in fact she was from the Midwest. Maybe her accent was picked up from her time in England, but doubtful. Who really cares though? With a life like hers, there was little to regret or poke fun at. She truly lived her life, every second of it.

Claudia reached for the photo album on the end table and flipped to the third page. "Here," she said and plopped it onto Audrey's lap. "Just a few were taken that summer, but you get the idea."

Sure enough, there she stood, eyes wild with passion,

The Purpose

hugging Sinatra. The next picture he was kissing her cheek while she sat on his lap. A love affair, indeed.

They spent the rest of the afternoon walking through the garden, whispering secrets of their past. Audrey unloaded the stories of Jason as they watered Gerber daisies and yellow daffodils poised in the sunlight. Claudia listened without judgment and when Audrey started to cry, she held her with strength and compassion. She lifted her chin and peered into her saddened eyes.

"My dear, you will find yourself again. Just give it time. But first, you need to forgive yourself."

* * * *

With a new sense of direction, Audrey spent the next week ripping open every box in her apartment and organizing it to the max. Her clothes were color-coded, her makeup arranged neatly in plastic containers, and even her several dozen shoes had special shelving. She sifted through boxes of papers, documents and bills to square them properly in files and folders. She hung pots and pans from dangling hooks in the kitchen and set up her square dining room table with votive candles and woven place mats.

A trip to the store with Claudia's car brought back new artwork, curtains and floral arrangements from the local thrift store. Her home was coming alive in vibrant shades of silver, hot pink and purple. For once, every purchase was selected by her and while she knew Emma would never approve of her modern and slightly juvenile taste, she loved it. She completed the living room with a single statue of a

The Purpose

porcelain woman with her arms outreached to the sky. Engraved on the bottom was "Go get it…" and it spoke to her.

Her bedroom came alive in classic black and white with glittering pillows against her patterned bedspread. Each nightstand held a lamp from Claudia with tear drop shaped Swarovski crystals lining the edge of the shade. August attempted only once to bat at them, before Audrey gave him a pat on the bottom. Stacks of books and magazines were neatly arranged on two ceiling height bookshelves and her laptop sat squarely on the built in desk in the living area. Her home was filled with pieces of her spirit and it never felt more like home.

Blake continued to call throughout the week, but Audrey politely refused his countless offers. He understood her needing to unpack and insisted on helping, but yet again she refused him. She knew he was enthralled by her, although she couldn't quite understand why. If he was truly interested, he would simply have to wait.

In the midst of hanging the last and largest portrait of the streets of Paris in her dining area, the picture titled slightly to the left, slamming her pinky finger behind it. The picture slid heavily to the floor with Audrey collapsing under it. As she lay there, flattened by the weight, she couldn't help but laugh and cry at the same time. She had done so well at arranging her whole apartment, but this picture would be the death of her. She called Emma, who respectfully declined with some sort of work emergency. Claudia was out for the evening and her parents were having

The Purpose

a dinner party. Her mother pressed for her to call Will as he was off this evening, but she refused. She refused Will and Blake and vowed to try again on her own.

Bandaging her finger, she heard an almost unnoticeable knock at the door. Will stood on the doorstep, looking nervous and frustrated.

"Your mom said you were having an emergency?"

Withholding a stifled laugh, she replied, "Hardly an emergency. I can't hang my Paris picture by myself. I can't believe she called you."

"She said you sounded like you were crying?"

"Whatever. Not even close, just frustrated. Come on in and thanks for coming I guess."

Will walked past her into her apartment, glancing top to bottom, left to right. He reached out and ran his fingers along her statue and touched the glimmering chandelier over the dining room table.

"This place. Wow." He laughed.

"I don't care what anyone thinks," she said. "I love it."

"No, that isn't what I meant. I mean, it is pretty incredible. Did you do all of this by yourself?"

"Yes I did." Her expression softened. "I have always wanted a place of my own."

"Well, you did a hell of a job. I mean a little girly for me, but it suits you. Looks like it is out of a magazine."

"Well, thanks, I guess. The picture is over here."

Will continued to look around in awe of every detail. He looked out the bay window into the garden. Although it was night time, it was still illuminated with a soft moonlight

The Purpose

glow. The willow tree swayed in the breeze and the flowers stood at perfect attention.

"Seriously, this place is amazing. How did you find it?"

"I work just down the street and I saw an ad in the coffee shop at the corner. You will have to meet my landlord Claudia. She sold me on the place."

Will went straight to work with the picture. She handed him the nails and he lifted it to eye level. She balanced one side as he marked the wall with pencil and then hammered in the nails. He propped the level on top of the picture once it was hung and stepped back with utter satisfaction.

"That'll do it." He smiled, wiping his hands against faded jeans.

"Gosh, that was really fast. I have been at this for about two hours. I can't thank you enough."

"For starters you can offer me something to drink."

"Oh? Well, aren't we demanding? All I have is wine."

"I'll take it."

They sat across from each other in the living room, Audrey on the couch, Will in the plush oversized purple arm chair, drinking their wine quietly. The clock in the background ticked loudly as they racked their brains for conversation, each nervous to discuss anything too personal.

"This is bullshit," Will blurted out.

"What is?" Audrey straightened up, alarmed.

"Us. We used to be like best friends, now we don't even know what to say to each other. Enough of the polite crap; tell me what happened with that jackass."

The Purpose

"I don't really want to…"

"Audrey, you can tell me. I won't judge you."

"Well, I hardly believe that, but if you really want to know."

"I do. Please."

"Well, you have to ask me certain questions to get me started, I guess." She nervously swirled the dark red wine in her glass, awaiting his reply.

"Okay, tell me when things got bad." His eyes pierced into her with sincerity and fear. He legitimately cared about her and wanted to know. She never believed he even knew about the situation. After all, they hadn't seen each other in years.

"Hold on." She lifted herself from the couch and grabbed the wine bottle. Topping off each glass, she settled in to his intense glare once more.

"Okay, here goes nothing…"

Will breathed the deepest breath and took a gulp of the sweet plum wine.

"We met when I was barely twenty years old. He pursued me like crazy. He was constantly calling, even writing me letters. After finally agreeing to go out with him, I fell head over heels. He was everything I had ever wanted: sweet, charming and crazy romantic. We moved in together way too fast. It had only been like three months of us dating and we got an apartment together. We decorated and played house with such ease in the beginning. We even got a cat." She pointed to August curled up at her feet.

"He would constantly leave me love notes, make me

The Purpose

dinner, and for no reason at all start dancing with me in the living room. I thought we were going to get married. I was starting my junior year in college when it got bad. He started having his friends over all of the time. They smoked pot in my living room and God knows what else when I wasn't around. He started talking down to me in front of them and flashes of anger came out of nowhere. Sometimes he would shove me because I didn't say the right thing or dress the right way. He was always so sorry, you know? He would apologize over and over and buy me things to try and make up for it. Those moments came so far in-between in the beginning, that looking back; I didn't even really notice a pattern at all. I chalked it up to being in a bad mood every now and again."

"The last six months were the worst. He would spit in my face, and throw things at me. He once even jumped on top of me and punched me in the head over and over again, forcing me to see stars. I never fought back, I was terrified. When I would try and stop him from driving when he was high, he would send me flying across the apartment with one shove. He kicked in the doors when I would try and hide from him. Our whole apartment was door-less, even the bathroom because of his temper. There wasn't anywhere to hide." She stopped for a moment to compose herself before continuing. Will continued to listen, never saying a word.

"His family was the worst. They kept telling me it was my fault that he was this way. There couldn't possibly be anything wrong with him. His mother, however, had always been abused by his father and had finally found the strength

The Purpose

to divorce him. She wanted me to leave him, I just knew it. I couldn't do it though. For whatever reason, I thought I could change him. I wanted to protect him and heal his hurting. His anger was coming from somewhere deep inside and I felt like he never meant to take it out on me."

"Do you still feel that way?" Will spoke out softly.

"No," she said forcefully. "Not even a little bit. I now know that there is something severely wrong with him mentally, and honestly, I feel sorry for him. No one can save him but himself, and probably some serious counseling and medication. You see, Will, when someone puts you down enough, you start to believe it and before you know it, you haven't got the strength to fight back or leave. He made me feel like he was the only person that could ever love me and I became desperate for his approval."

"I always wondered how women, even strong women like yourself, could stay in a relationship like that."

"I was just lucky to have gotten out. We didn't have any children and weren't married, so it was a clean break. However, if it hadn't been his decision to leave, I am not sure I ever would have. I was so weak and alone and when he finally took off, I counted the seconds until he returned."

"Really?"

"Yeah, that is how Emma found me. She didn't know the half of it at that time, but only thought he was a little verbally abusive. Now that she truly gets it, she is appalled at what I consciously chose to live through. No one will ever understand it until they deal with it. I didn't understand what love was, and I certainly didn't love myself. He always

The Purpose

pointed out flaws in my family and tried to turn me against them. That is what a lot of abusive men do. They alienate you from everyone you love to the point of feeling so dependent on them. They want to be the only source of any emotion or life in your world and once they completely have you that is when they manipulate you and screw with your head. It took me a while to see through his lies and to believe that family is the only true people I can actually trust. Now that I have found my way back home, I will never get lost again." She closed her eyes as tears welled up and overflowed on to her cheeks.

Will sat completely still, unsure of what to say or do.

"You can hug me if you want," she said, choking on her sobs.

He rushed across the living room, sat down, and scooped her onto his lap, rocking her back and forth. "Oh, Audrey," he whispered. "I wish I would have known."

She didn't care that she was being vulnerable. She had always cherished her relationship with Will. He used to bandage her cuts when they were little, playing near the creek, and had always protected her on the playground. Sometimes a weak moment can put a friendship right back where it needs to be. More than anything, she needed to get this story out. Will was right, it had been eating her alive and suddenly it was if a large boulder had been lifted from on top of her.

Another glass of wine had Will spilling about his time in medical school and his only girlfriend in college. Audrey had wiped her tears and was actually laughing out loud as

The Purpose

he recounted his first experience in surgery. He made hand gestures, imitated voices and told story after story until he had her rolling on the floor with laughter. As Will reached for a new bottle off the wine rack, they jumped out of their skin when her Paris picture crashed to the ground. It took a moment to register, but their laughter roared once more at the sight.

They talked through the night and fell asleep on opposite ends of the couch with their socks touching as the sun came up. August kept their feet warm by lying flat on top in the center. It was the most peaceful and comfortable sleep Audrey had in ages. The sense of belonging and friendship swirled around in her dreams and for once, she felt truly relaxed.

* * * *

A mere four hours later, the sun was bursting through the bay window, making it impossible to sleep another wink. Will rolled off the couch, wrapped a blanket around Audrey and slipped out the front door. On his way, he ran smack into the most interesting woman he had ever met. Through her bright red lipstick, Claudia said, "You must be Blake?"

"Oh no actually...I'm Will."

"Will? Audrey never mentioned you. Don't mind me though. You two kids have fun."

Will continued his journey to the coffee shop, his mind ever present on the doll-like woman from the hall. Audrey was with Blake, it was pretty clear. Yet, he didn't think she

The Purpose

was ready. Not yet. She was still entirely too emotional and needed some time to herself; time to heal. He needed to tell her that. Someone had to look out for her after all. Two French vanilla cappuccinos and two blueberry scones should set the tone for his forthcoming opinions.

He trudged back down the hill and into the apartment to find her still sleeping. He couldn't help but watch her for only a moment, recounting how sad she had been. She wasn't the same girl she had always been. She used to be so strong, impossible almost. Now, she was every bit of frailty and fear. He struggled with his inability to say the right thing or be there for her during those difficult months, but his father had mentioned so little, saying instead that she had a jerk of a boyfriend and hadn't been coming around much. No one truly knew the half of it until it was over and the damage had been done.

He reached out and tucked a blonde curl behind her ear. Her makeup was smudged and he caught a glimpse of the ten-year-old version of her that used to sit in the highest of branches and throw acorns at him from the treetops. He would get so angry at her, part annoyance and part fear of her falling. She would laugh incessantly and mock his demands for her to get down. She had never listened to him back then and most likely wouldn't now, but he had to try.

She stirred slightly to find August lying on her hip, staring at her.

"Hi, buddy," she said and smiled. "My head is killing me."

"Mine, too," Will grumbled from the kitchen. He

The Purpose

reached for a plate and a butter knife to cut the scones apart.

"Oh, hey, Will. I thought you had left." She stretched to the ceiling with an exaggerated yawn.

"No, we need to talk." He never really was good at timing.

"Can I go to the bathroom first?" she mocked.

"Sure."

He brought the coffee cups and scones into the living room and set them on top of the treasure chest coffee table. Carefully he sliced open the scones and gingerly applied butter on either side.

Sliding into her slippers, she returned to the living room and hopped under the covers. "What's up?" She reached for a scone. "Yum, thanks."

"You can't date this Blake guy."

"Um, good morning to you too. What are you talking about?"

"You're just not ready. You are so far from ready it is unreal and if you push yourself into another relationship this fast, you are going to regret it."

"Where is this coming from? Why are you so upset?"

"I just worry about you and after last night, I saw this situation for what it really is. You need to allow yourself some time."

"And what is this situation?" Her eyes narrowed.

"Don't misunderstand me. The situation I am referring to is likely a bad spell you are going through. You'll get over it eventually."

"I'll get over it? That's what you think? Like it is a

hangover or something? Come on, Will, we had a great night of confiding as friends. Don't ruin that."

He hesitated before continuing, "You're not getting what I am saying. He just isn't what you need right now."

"I will be fine, Will. You can't suddenly be my protector now."

"I'm….gonna go. Sorry." He put down his scone and headed for the door. "Just remember there is all the time in the world and when you are ready the right guy will be there waiting."

Chapter 6

"Why is he such a pain in the ass?" Audrey screeched into the phone at Emma. "We have this awesome night of laughter and it felt just like the old days. Then the sun comes up and he is back into his old, proverbial ways, like an evil Cinderella."

"You can't help but see his point just a little bit though, right, Bear?" Emma pushed back. "I mean, maybe I did force you too fast into this whole Blake thing. Maybe you should take a little more time to yourself."

"You guys are impossible. And no, you are not right. The days of Jason are behind me and I need to start living again."

She hung up with Emma wondering if she even believed herself. After all, they say it takes twice the amount of time to get over someone as the amount of time you were with them. Considering they were dating for a year all together, then she needed two years to get over him? Sweet

The Purpose

Lord! With that kind of time, she would surely die of loneliness. She only needed a distraction to get her through for a while. Blake surely couldn't be her true love, but merely a chance at a quick and lively love affair, like Claudia and Frank. With that notion, she promptly dialed Blake and invited him to join her for a more simplistic date. This time, she called the shots and that meant no grand gestures, only dinner and a movie.

* * * *

At the shelter the next morning, she was greeted by a huge bouquet of white lilies with a note that read, "*More beautiful than the loveliest lily. ~Blake*" Why wasn't she surprised? Their date was scheduled for this evening and he was already starting in with the dramatic attention. For some reason, it bothered her. Maybe it was a little bit of the Jason thing, seeing as they started out exactly the same way with overwhelming romance. The receptionist eyed her with curiosity as she stuffed the note in her pocket and moved the flowers to the entry table.

"You don't want to put those in your office?" she asked.

"No thanks, keep them here. They will make the lobby smell better." Her lame response only made the act more embarrassing. She shuffled back to dog pins and said her good mornings. This was her routine. There wasn't a puppy in the room that didn't get a hello and a pat to start the day. One by one she instructed the volunteers how to undo cages and get their leashes on snug without too much pull. The

The Purpose

yellow Labrador watched with interest from the last cage as she made her way down the aisle. There were exactly sixteen dogs in the shelter today and they ranged from teacup Chihuahuas to a Mastiff of large proportion.

Once she was finished with the more animated dogs, she moved to the cat house to greet each of the nineteen felines in the shelter. She had placed a little catnip in her pocket and they went crazy fighting for her attention. She moved quickly to fill dishes of food and water alongside the volunteers and then left them to the additional morning routine. It was time to open up shop and even more so, they were preparing for a large adoption event at the end of the month. There were plans of a "Family Fur Fest" at the shelter, to be equipped with horseback riding, kettle corn, clowns and, of course, plenty of adoptions. She intended to find homes for over half of her animals and raise awareness on the conditions of animal cruelty, as Missouri is one of the states with the least amount of regulations of puppy mills and other forms of abuse.

Tucked back in her office, she awaited any pages of visitors looking for a new friend from the front. In the meantime, she had plenty of paperwork to file and emails to check. She reached behind her to put her long hair into a high ponytail to get it out of her face and re-laced one of her work boots. *If only Blake could see her now—man, was she polished.*

An hour into her work load, a call from the front found her face to face with an all too familiar past. She heard his voice from the back and gasped before rushing out to see him. There he stood, looking more trim and strong than ever. His hair was longer than usual and his face appeared worn out and exhausted. When his eyes focused on her, he stood transfixed.

"What are you doing here, Jason? How did you even know where I work?"

"Is that anyway to say hello? Now get over here and give me a hug." He reached his arms forward, instantly angry when she took a step backwards.

"What do you want?" she said and glared.

"Just missing you a little, that's all. Can't we talk for a minute?"

"We have nothing to talk about; you need to go."

His eyes flashed with flames. "Well, you see that isn't happening. I went by our old place and all your stuff was gone. Did you leave and not even tell me? They are expecting me to pay a pretty hefty fee to break that lease and there ain't no way in hell I am paying for it. I'll wait while you get some cash."

"Why should I have to pay for that? You left before I did."

"Listen, bitch." He stepped closer to her, putting his face in hers. "Get the money, now."

The receptionist gasped before running to the back of the shelter. *Thank you*, Audrey thought, *for leaving me alone with him.*

He grabbed her arm and tried one more time. "Now!"

She tried to pull away but his grip held firm. "How much is it?" She felt herself crumble from fear. "I don't

The Purpose

have any money with me right now."

"Six hundred dollars. I will be here at nine tomorrow to get it from you. If you don't have it, well, something might just 'happen' to your little shelter here. Figure it out."

With that he was gone and Audrey stood trembling. How had he found her? Where was she going to get the money? Would he really do something to the shelter? The last question was a ridiculous one. He would probably torch the place and not even think twice, and as usual she had no way to prove it. Her mind raced immediately with anyone she could possibly ask. She hated ever asking anything of her family. She still felt so indebted to them in the first place. They would never give her the money to begin with if they knew why she needed it. Maybe Claudia could loan it to her? She would pay her back of course, but she didn't want to ask.

* * * *

"Oh darling, I would surely love to help you, but I just don't have that kind of money."

Audrey stood in front of Claudia, shaking in her boots. How had her life come to this? How did he still have such a hold over her?

Forcing herself not to cry, she smiled and nodded. "I figured, Claudia, I am just terrified. The shelter is such a special place to me and it scares me to death. I would never ask if there wasn't anyone else in this world that could help me. I am so sorry I even asked this of you." The tears fell against her better judgment and Claudia hugged her tightly.

The Purpose

"What about that young man, Will was it? He seemed very friendly."

"Oh God no, he would never lend me money for this reason. Plus, he would never let me live it down. Maybe I can sell something?"

"Dear, I have seen your apartment and it is pretty bare bones. Perhaps I have something you can sell." Claudia looked around her room, eyeing various antiques.

"Absolutely not," Audrey rushed. "Thank you anyway."

She trudged up the stairs, her mind going a thousand miles a minute. Maybe Will was her only option. She had exactly one hour before she was supposed to meet Blake, so she had to move quickly. Dressing herself in under five minutes, she was out the door in a cab to the hospital in little to no time at all.

* * * *

Walking slowly through the hospital halls, she was reminded of her recent visit. She had been meaning to volunteer, but once again her life got in the way of any good doing she had intended. Tomorrow, she would certainly call. The volunteer at the front desk paged Will with a quiet voice and told her to have a seat. She collapsed into the plush couch and waited and waited. After forty-five minutes, Will came breezing through the halls in his blue surgical scrubs once again. He stared at her with inquisitiveness as he crossed the lobby. Running his fingers through his hair, they spoke at the exact same time.

The Purpose

"I'm sorry," Will said.

"I need a favor…" Audrey countered.

"What? You go first. What's going on?" He looked worried.

"Can we talk for a minute? Maybe in the cafeteria or something?"

"Uh sure, I only have about fifteen minutes before my next round. Follow me."

The stretch of the hallway seemed incredulously long as she envisioned how to ask this of him. It was Will, for crying out loud. He had always been there for her.

He swiped his badge, purchasing two coffees, and escorted her to a table off to the side of the busy café. Families crowded around the scores of fresh salad, pizza and baked chicken. Children reached high on the candy rack, begging for more treats, while their parents, looking tired and overwhelmed, shooed them away.

She was dazing in and out of focus when Will asked, "What's up, Audrey? Talk to me."

In slow and overly dramatic detail, she recounted the story from that afternoon. Will listened intently and his face went white when she told him of his threat.

"You have to call the police," he replied instantly.

"And say what exactly, that he is demanding I help pay for a termination fee that technically I guess I should be helping with? They can't do anything and it is my word against his. It is best that I pay the fee and close him out of my life, for good," she said sternly.

"Until next time," Will muttered. "So, you need my

The Purpose

money to help you pay? Is that what you are getting at?"

"Please, Will, I promise to pay you back as soon as I can. I can't ask my parents; they'll threaten him and they will never give me the money if they know where it is going. It absolutely, gut-wrenching kills me that I have to ask you this, but please, please…"

"Stop," he said calmly. "Follow me to the ATM."

Her eyes softened and she filled with hope. "You would do this for me?"

"On one condition." He turned toward her. "I want to be with you tomorrow when he comes for it."

The look in his eyes told her just how much he meant it and she retracted her upcoming statement. "Okay," she said simply. He gave her six hundred even and walked her to the lobby.

"See you at nine." He gave a grin and kissed the top of her head.

She tucked the money safely into her purse and hailed another cab to the restaurant to meet Blake. The same young-adult looking hostess greeted her as the other night, this time with long straightened hair instead. "Audrey right?" she said and smiled.

"Yes, is Blake here already?"

"Sure is! Follow me." Audrey followed her through crowds of couples and families dining in the restaurant. There was a low hum of chatter over candlelight, wine and pasta that only encouraged her nerves. The hostess pulled her chair out and she slid in and locked eyes with Blake—gorgeous green eyes.

The Purpose

"Well, look who is feeling better." He reached out and rubbed his hand along her forearm. Without realizing it, she pulled back and pretended to straighten her napkin and placemat.

"Thank you again for the other night." She looked down. "I am feeling much better."

"Well, let's not dwell on it and have a lovely evening. I am so glad you called me and asked me to meet you."

The waiter greeted them, a young man of about eighteen years of age with spiky blond hair. His white apron hung low around his waist with specks of red marinara sauce splashed in various spots. He offered specials: chicken spadini with angel hair pasta or four-cheese stuffed ravioli with a prosciutto cream sauce. He poured a 2008 Merlot per Blake's request and left the bottle at the table. The candle cast a warm glow, highlighting Blake's cheekbones and tiny gold flecks in his eyes. He talked continuously about work, his family and at last his feelings for her. As he spoke, she felt herself nodding and smiling in all the right places, but lacking any real interest in what he was saying. He was beautiful, there was no denying that, but her mind was elsewhere and it was not even remotely fair for him. The food arrived in record time and she continued to peer in on their date as an outsider would with Blake talking enough for the both of them.

"I would like to propose a toast." Blake raised his glass. "To knowing when there is something special and refusing to let it go. You, my sweet Audrey, are so very special."

His glass hung in the air as she stood frozen, staring at

The Purpose

it. "Um, Audrey, the toast?" he reminded her.

"Oh, yes." She lifted the long-stemmed wine glass to gently press it against his with a soft ringing sound. "You are pretty special too," she replied, recovering the awkward moment in a charming afterthought.

The evening continued with Crème Brule and a desert wine. She opened up about her childhood and her relationship with Emma and her parents when he asked her a minimum of twelve questions in a row, while he sat entranced by her every sentence.

"So you and Will grew up together?" he asked. *Thirteen.*

"Yeah, his house is right behind my parents and we used to play by the pond and around in the woods. You know, typically just kid stuff, building forts and what not."

"Sounds fun. It is nice to have a childhood friend still in your life today. Do you guys see each other much anymore?" *Fourteen.*

"I don't know if I would say 'in my life', as much as more so recently. He is a good guy though." She felt the conversation leaning toward his interest in her relationship with Will. "Why do you ask?"

"I just like learning about you, that's all. What do you say we get out of here?" Finally, a question she had been waiting for.

"Sounds great." *Something, anything to ease the tension*, she thought.

The night air hit her with a rush of relief, forcing the sounds of the restaurant to the back of her mind. Every

The Purpose

cloud in existence was out tonight, covering even the brightest star. While she waited for Blake to pay the waiter, she rocked back and forth on her heals, gazing at the sky. The moon was bursting with silver light and outlined each cloud, making them seem 3D and almost alive as they rolled through the darkness. She pictured herself floating through them, escaping every bit of fear she was feeling. He would be there at nine, and so would Will. What on earth would Will do or say? If they got into a fight, she pictured Will winning. He was much taller than Jason, and had forearms not expected on a doctor. Jason was scrappy though, scrawny but vicious.

"You ready?" Blake placed his hand at the small of her back and led her to his car. "You feeling okay? You seem pretty quiet."

"To be honest, I am worn out. We have so much going on at the shelter, and there will be even more drama tomorrow. Any way I can take a rain check on the movie?" She didn't look at him. She knew he was crushed. This was officially her bailing or withdrawing, so to speak, from their second date. More than likely he would never call her again after tonight. She wouldn't if she were him. After all, he had a lot of self confidence and didn't seem like the type to be screwed around with. She heard him sigh and forced herself to look into his eyes.

"I had a wonderful time tonight. You are wonderful. Rain check, promise?" His answers were so scripted, as if a tiny man were sitting inside his pocket feeding him the straight from the cinema lines to make even her swoon. Not

The Purpose

to mention the way his eyes crinkled when he smiled, like they had seen hours of hysterical moments that only he would ever know of.

"Promise." She nodded.

He let her out at the door, walked her up to the doorstep and without saying a word, he reached for her hand and lightly kissed the tip of her knuckles. "Sweet dreams, gorgeous."

Once inside, she rammed her head against the door, which no doubt he heard, repeating, "Stupid, stupid…stupid woman…" *Wham!*

Chapter 7

At exactly, 8:59 a.m., the door to the shelter flung open with extra-strength, revealing the most real-life version of a villain Audrey had ever known. Smoke might as well have been coming out of his ears and his eyes veiled over with a red curtain. He marched, hands fisted into a ball, straight toward her. She waited whatever was to come, pretending this was all a dream. It wasn't. He was real and somehow still so intricately woven into her existence. Will was running late and it was eating her alive. Jason was not the kind of man you can stall with bullshit or small talk.

"Well?" he hissed.

"We need to talk first." *Be brave, be brave.* "You see, I need you to understand that I am not the same person you left last winter. I have thought long and hard what I would ever say to you if I had the chance." She paused to see if what she was saying was registering.

"So, I could care less," he started.

"Let her talk!" Will flung open the door with all his strength, sending it flying against the doorstop with a loud crack.

"Who is this guy?" Jason rolled his eyes.

"Go on." Will slipped his arm around her shoulder, staring Jason dead in the eye.

She shuddered at the intensity of everything around her. Fear started to overcome her again, but she took a deep breath and continued feeling Will's strength merging within her. "I just want to say that I see now why you left. What we had was the most disturbing illustration of a relationship to ever walk this earth. The way you think of love is so far removed from the real thing, it makes me sad. You are abusive, Jason, and I deserve better." With the last word, she puffed up her chest and reached into her pocket.

"No, hold on a second." Will put his hand on her arm. "This is not how this is going to go down."

"Look, dude, if you are searching for a fight, I am all yours." Jason stepped toward Will, within three inches of his face, his signature move.

"The money will be returned to the landlord at your old apartment. We have every bit of six hundred dollars here, but there is no way in hell that I trust you to return it to him. I will follow you to the apartment and hand it to him myself. From there, you are never to set foot in this place or bother Audrey again. Your bullying days are done, *dude*. This is

The Purpose

the final string that connects you two."

Audrey stood in awe. Who was this guy? He was strong, forceful, and she had never felt so protected before. She studied Will's face, his gritted teeth making his jaw clench. His eyes were full of anger and yet, there was something so childlike about his battle stance.

"Whatever, *dude*," said Jason and he withdrew. "I am done with this bitch anyway."

Will stopped himself from lunging forward, remembering the importance of making him go away for good, not stirring the pot to agitate him further.

"I would jack you in your face, but I have a feeling it wouldn't teach you a lesson of any sort." Will turned toward Audrey. "Stay here and I will be back within a half hour."

While Will was talking, Jason stood behind him with a look of shear satisfaction, his middle finger proudly hung on display.

* * * *

Audrey kept herself busy cleaning at the shelter while she waited. It had always been her way of coping. For instance, when she was seven years old and had joined Will on a mission to save the children of Africa. They had spent hours plotting how they could raise enough money to sponsor a child for a whole year. At $91.25, or rather twenty-five cents a day, they could provide shelter, education and something about vaccinations to an innocent child in need. Will had seen the commercial on television and swore up and down, although his father would kill him

The Purpose

if he knew he was swearing on anything, that this is what they were meant to do.

"It says so in the Bible." He frowned at her. "We have to do it."

She questioned him, not because he wanted to save the world with her as his partner in crime, but because his only way of raising money settled on "collecting" from family members.

"Dad always leaves a penny jar in the kitchen; he will never know. Plus, Nanna usually has rolls of quarters in paper wrapping tucked away in her pantry."

He insisted she take it upon herself to search through her parents things and come up with at least a third of the money. All reservations aside, she began digging. She turned up eight dollars from her sister's penny bank, twenty dollars from her father's ash tray in the car and sixty-seven dollars and twenty-two cents in her mother's wallet. She knew her life would be over if they ever knew it had been her that took it. Feeling nervous, anxious and even a little bit proud, she tossed the money on the pegged table in their clubhouse, watching Will's eyes light up with wonder.

"Where on earth? I can't believe you did it!" Will had jumped up and down, never blinking for what seemed like hours. "You raised all of it by yourself, you little scoundrel."

She remembered hearing the word, knowing it was meant of pure affection, but hating it all the same. She was not a thief, she didn't know how to walk, talk or think like one, and the money was staring up at her like those innocent children on the

The Purpose

commercial. Her parents would surely disown her; maybe even send her to Africa to live like these children to learn the value of a dollar. She would be denied food, deprived of clothing and would never even learn what a vaccination was.

"I can't do it." She put her head down and started to cry deep heaving sobs. Will stood idly by, unsure whether to hug her or punch her in the shoulder.

"Don't...don't cry," he stuttered. "We can return it and find another way."

They gathered the money back into her pink lacy sock she had brought it in and Will followed her back up to the house. They confessed everything to her mother with overly dramatic renditions of how they were only trying to save the world. When they finished, Will laid the pink sock onto the kitchen table and quietly put his arm around Audrey. "I made her do it, Mrs. Landrow. Please don't punish her."

Despite her best efforts, Audrey's mother broke out into laughter, saying, "You two kids never cease to amaze me with your wild ideas. Thank you for returning the money and know that I am proud of you at the same time as I am furious with you. Will, you are an endearing boy for trying to stand up for my little bear, but you must know that she is her own person and can take care of herself, including making decisions on her own. No one in this world can force her into doing anything she doesn't want to do. So with that said, she will be grounded for precisely one week. Go on home, now."

The entire seven days, Audrey spent organizing, dusting, arranging, sweeping the whole house, not because

The Purpose

her mother asked her to, but instead because she was desperate to rid herself of the awful way she felt. If possible, she intended to cleanse her filthy soul.

* * * *

Knee deep inside a kennel with a blonde-haired poodle peering preciously in on her from the next, Audrey felt a firm foot gently pushing her bottom to one side, forcing her to lose her balance and land flat on the concrete floor. Flipping over to her side, she saw Will gazing at her with pure amusement, stifling a laugh. "Cleaning, I see," he said.

Army crawling out of the cage, she closed it behind her and stood up to meet him eye level. "It kills you to be nice for too long." She slipped of her gloves and tossed them on top of the cage. "Well, what happened? Did he say anything else?"

Will was still laughing when he reached out to smooth the side of her hair down. "You just look so damn lovely." He smirked.

"Seriously, Will. Come on. What the hell happened?"

"Not much, I followed him there, paid the landlord and came back here. Oh, but the balance was actually only two-fifty to break the lease. Nice try, jackass."

"Seriously, so he was just gonna keep the rest for himself? Is that what you're saying?" She peered at him anxiously.

"Yep, he didn't even try and say that he thought it was six hundred dollars. What a piece of work."

"So how did you leave things? Did you say anything else to him?"

The Purpose

"Nah, just told him I meant what I said, about leaving you alone. He answered something like, 'yeah, yeah', which where I come from means, 'Okay'. You should be good from here on out—seems like he only wanted his money."

Before Will could finish explaining, Audrey had reached up to wrap her arms around his neck. She hugged him for a long time, exclaiming, "Thank you, thank you, thank you…" until finally she crawled down off him and stood there, embarrassed by her outburst of affection.

"Well, aren't you quite the emotional mess." He fixed her hair again. The tension between them eased away and the laughter returned. She showed him around the kennel, introducing each animal by name and shared several of their stories with him. When they came to the last cage on the right, Will's eyes zeroed in on a Siberian husky with the sharpest blue eyes he'd ever seen.

"Who is this?" he asked with a little too much eagerness.

"His name is Freedom," she gushed. "We just got him yesterday. Look at those eyes."

"Freedom, huh? I like it. Do you think someone will adopt him? Shame to see such an awesome dog in here alone in a cage." Will's eyes glazed over as he reached through the cage to feel Freedom's nose. It was so warm, like a muffin straight from the oven. It wiggled when he touched it and sent out soft bursts of air. Sticking it all the way through the cage bars, his blue eyes drooped slightly at the touch.

"He gets out pretty often; we have play dates and go for long walks. Would you like me to get him out for you?"

The Purpose

"Maybe another time." Will straightened up, clearing his throat, and turned back to Audrey. He knew what she was trying to do; after all it was her job. "I thought for now we could go grab a coffee if you have a second."

"Sure, let me wash my hands and grab my purse."

Freedom continued to rub against the cage and started a gentle whine that came from a dark and lonely place. Will's heart wrenched and he pulled his hand back and forced himself to walk away. Freedom would find a good home, no doubt. He was in the best hands, after all.

"I have a favor to ask of you, now." Will took a long drawl of his piping hot coffee.

"Anything, just name it." Audrey couldn't help but wonder if this was the very reason he agreed to help her. He needed something in return.

"Promise you will do what I ask? I really need this favor bad."

"Will." She lowered her eyebrows. The coffee shop was completely empty other than the pencil thin older man behind the counter with skin-tight plaid shirt, jeans and a rather intense mustache. Audrey felt her gaze drift between the serious Will and the comical coffee man.

"Okay, okay, here it is." He paused. "I need you to forget about repaying the money. Seriously, Audrey, I want you to consider it a gift. You have worked so hard to get where you are and I know that you are climbing your way back out. I have never seen you take money from anyone and it kills you to do so, but I want to do this for you. So, there you have it, *my* favor."

The Purpose

Will continued to sip his coffee as the mustache-coffee man began to whistle. Fighting every urge she had to scream out, "I don't need you, I am not a charity case," she lowered her head and stared into the swirling cream beginning to form a tornado shape.

"On one condition," she mumbled.

"Hey, how did you just switch this on me?" Will questioned. "You are supposed to be doing me a favor."

"Well, you see, it is an awful lot to ask. I can help you out, but I am going to need something in return," she said and smirked.

"Anything." He leaned forward, locking eyes with her.

The coffee-mustache-plaid-shirt man stopped whistling.

"You have to take Freedom home with you today." Her gaze never faltered and her voice held firm.

Will erupted into laughter, almost spilling his coffee. "Got to hand it to you, kid, you are brilliant. Fine, whatever it takes, but where the hell is he supposed to go when I head to England in a couple of months?"

"You mean it? You'll take him? He is perfect for you, I just knew it. I will take care of him while you are gone, promise."

"Yeah, yeah," said Will and smiled.

A half hour later, Freedom bounded out of the kennel, trotting alongside Will, tongue hanging out and eyes filled with light in the sunshine. Audrey waved from the front door and watched as Freedom hopped up into Will's truck and took his seat next to him as if that is where he had always belonged.

* * * *

The Purpose

Further buried deep in paperwork later that afternoon, her phone started to ring. It was the hospital returning her call about volunteering. Somehow she had managed to remember, despite that morning's events. She had hoped to tell Will, wondering if he could believe she would, just to be around him. He was quickly redeeming their friendship, but that wasn't the reason. This was something she needed to do on her own, for her alone. Claudia's words continued to reverberate in her ears, "find your purpose," as if it were some sort of mantra she desperately clung to. Feeling so lost in the last few years, she knew it was time. Time to firmly plant her feet on the ground into something real, something she could be proud of.

"Hello?" She answered the ringing phone.

"Is this Audrey?"

"Yes, this is she."

"My name is Elaine, I am calling from Barnes-Jewish Hospital and would like to discuss a volunteer position with you after receiving your application online. Do you have any idea what area you might be interested in?"

She smiled into the phone, exhaled and said, "Absolutely, the women's center if it is available. I need to give back the many blessings in my life by helping encourage other women to be strong during their struggles in life."

"Hmm, let me see," said Elaine, while shuffling through a stack of papers in the background. "I think I have just the position for you. It is for three hours every Friday afternoon, starting at three. Your application said you get off work at 2:30?"

"Perfect."

The Purpose

* * * *

"Don't you think you have enough on your plate?" questioned Emma. "I mean, you can't even stay awake for a movie with Blake."

Emma sat cross-legged in the middle of the oversized couch at Audrey's apartment, stuffing chips into her cheeks. With the word, 'plate' precisely six pieces of chips flew across the coffee table at Audrey, who was currently hovering in the *downward dog* yoga pose.

"Emma, come on. I appreciate the set-up, really I do, but I need to do some things for me now. Dating is not going to be the priority for me."

"And I am proud of you, don't get me wrong, but I don't want to see you burn out on this new adventure of yours."

"What adventure? Life? Is that what you are referring to?"

Emma reached for her soda, crumpling the potato chip bag into an empty ball on the end table. Her messy blonde hair was twisted into a knot at the nape of her neck making her cheeks look especially puffy. No makeup, yoga pants and small pieces of chips woven into her shirt pulled together the perfect '*I'm not trying...even a little bit*' look she obviously was attempting.

"Mom and dad are just a little worried about you. They said Will has been coming around to watch over you, claiming you seem 'lost' or something."

With that, Audrey dropped out of her pose, wiped the

The Purpose

sweat from above her eyebrows and glared at Emma. "Lost!" she huffed. "He said I am lost? Screw him."

"Not like that, don't take it so personally. He worries about you, like a big brother, always has. Calm down."

There was something about every man that Audrey had always tried to connect the dots between. For years, they always seemed the same, no matter how much effort they put into changing. Regardless of the way they came across, they always looked down on her, like they had to help her. Poor little Audrey could never fend for herself, could never do anything on her own. Sure, Will had come to her rescue, but now she regretted ever even allowing him to hang that picture in her apartment, which he did a lousy job at. He knew she needed him and he played into her weakness, boasting to everyone around them that he was her knight in shining armor.

Emma, unrelenting, kept chowing down, this time on a box of chocolates she had brought over for Audrey. Taking little notice of any of the rainbow of emotions shooting across Audrey's face, she continued, "Anyways, you are not the daughter he should be worried about."

"Why would he worry about you? You have never had any issues, ever," she said with a tinge too much resentment.

"Because…I am pregnant," she said through a mouthful of chocolate. Audrey leapt across the living room and smothered Emma with hugs and kisses from her sweet filled cheeks to her barely there belly.

"Oh my gosh! I can't believe it!"

They spent the next hour rehashing every detail from

the moment she peed on a stick to the moment she told Alex. He was climbing the ladder to fix the gutter on the side of the house as it had worked itself loose when she blared out against the wind, "You're gonna be a dad!" He gripped the ladder within seconds of falling and started to cry from the top rung. They were going baby room paint shopping this weekend and picking out cribs on Sunday. She was only three months along, but due date couldn't come fast enough. They had been trying for over a year and half now.

They literally had the perfect life, right down to their relationship. Alex was constantly eager to please, attentive to her feelings and in touch with her every emotion. He was by far, the definition of what marriage should and could be. They had met in college, him hell-bent on becoming the best lawyer anyone had ever seen, with goals of moving up to Judge status later in life and her with a childhood dream of helping people. He spent hundreds of hours in the library, while she did internships on counseling and when the schooling had finally ceased, they found themselves with only one thing left to do, get married and find the dream house in the suburbs. Their wedding was a flawless evening in a silk tent under the stars. They were married during the spring with tulips as her only flower and she was covered in their grandmother's diamonds when she walked down the aisle in a fitted Vera Wang strapless sequin gown. Audrey watched on as the maid of honor with envy and adoration wondering if her life would ever even come close to that kind of perfection. Now three years later, their life was

The Purpose

complete with beautiful babies to come. Jealousy was last thing on her mind as she listened in wonderment of her sister's pregnancy. This is what she deserved. Her sister was the kindest person she had ever known, right down to her passion for the children she guided. She spoke constantly of them with tears in her eyes, rehashing every scornful detail of their trying situations. On many occasions, she had even taken a child into her home when their parents struggled with financial or medical issues. Her walls were filled with *Employee of the Month* and *Compassion at its Finest* awards demonstrating her call to life had been the fitting choice.

    Any form of frustration, irritation or anger drifted away as Audrey lay awake that night thinking of Emma. This is what life was about, days like this one. There are so few miracles intertwined with the complications of this world. Finally a moment of pure bliss, and she didn't intend on wasting it on hiccups and irrational assumptions. Maybe Will was right, she did need help. It was time to be open to letting people in to stand by you through the crooked course. She was like a newly born fawn, unsteady and nervous. He had done nothing other than hold her up when she needed it most and she was getting stronger each and every day. Tomorrow, she would tell Will thank you, Blake goodbye and start experiencing life on her own terms. God only gave her one life and she intended to live every ounce of it.

Chapter 8

Audrey lay awake waiting for the alarm to go off by six o'clock in the morning. Finally, she reached over and switched the off button at 5:45 a.m. No sense in putting off the inevitable. She had made a vow to herself last night, time to put her first, time to find her purpose. Making her way out of her apartment, she slid a handwritten note under Claudia's door with *"Your Ball has been rescheduled, my dear. In the garden next Friday evening at 7p.m. Don't be late!"*

Next she headed to the hospital to make her peace with Will. Once again they paged him and when he found her in the lobby, she gave him another handwritten note that read, *"I owe you one. Meet me at my apartment tomorrow night for a surprise."*

He held the note in his hand, anxious to read it, but she insisted he wait until she left. Stealing the confidence of Blake's winking concept, she sent one in his direction as she ran out of the hospital.

The Purpose

Her next stop took her to the florist, where she bought the biggest bouquet of white tulips they had in stock. On the note tucked in the flowers, she wrote, *"You are my inspiration, Love Audrey."* She left them at the receptionist desk for Emma and headed off to her next destination.

Standing in front of Blake's law office, she took a deep breath and climbed the stairs to the entrance. He was finishing up a meeting, so she sat in with Alex for a moment, gushing over the details of his fatherhood to come. Blake poked his head in on them and smiled. "Hey, gorgeous." This was going to be harder than she thought.

"Hey, there. Gotta sec?"

"All the time in the world for you," he said and smiled. *Damn those lines*!

She followed him down a hall of wooden paneling to his office tucked in the back corner. The room was filled with windows overlooking a large lake in the background. His office boasted trinkets from his many travels: a Buda, Tiki man, painted plates from the Dominican and a small replica of the Eifel Tower. Settling into his large leather chair, she found herself face to face again with those fierce green eyes.

"What's on your mind?" he asked.

She inhaled and then let it out, let every piece of her inhibitions go. "Blake, I have been struggling with our dates."

"Ouch." He looked hurt.

"No, not because they aren't picture perfect out of a book; even my hospital visit with you was a tale to be told.

The Purpose

It is just that for once I am standing on my own two feet, you know? Finally, I am breathing in my own right. I know that you don't know the whole story with my ex, or what I have really been through, but you would understand so much more if you did."

Blake sat with his head in his hands, listening at full attention. There was no one else in the world other than her right now.

"I only need some time for me, right now, that is all. You are by far the most perfect man I have ever met in real life, but if I don't take this chance to figure things out, I will more than likely lose myself in someone again. I can't be that girl, I won't be. I want to try new things, travel and really laugh again. Am I making any sense?"

"Perfect sense. Audrey, there is nothing in this world I want more than to see you happy. If you are meant to be with me, your wind will point you in my direction again someday. Anything I can do for you?"

"Really, just like that? Thank you, thank you for understanding. And maybe just one thing…"

"Anything, name it."

"Can you tell Emma?"

He laughed, flashing his white teeth and forcing his one and only dimple to show. "Of course." He smiled. "My pleasure."

She stood, allowing the leather chair to make an awkward sound causing her to blush, straightened out her bohemian skirt and extended her arms out to him. He accepted and they hugged for only a moment. Before

The Purpose

closing the door, she turned back and said, "Goodbye, gorgeous," before offering a wink. She heard him laugh again as she walked out the door of the office.

Her last and final stop of her daily mission took her to Webster University, home of the best undergrad education she could have asked for. Stealing two minutes with the guidance counselor, she found herself face to face with several options for a graduate program. There was the option to pursue creative writing and write the book she had always wanted to do. Or, she was considering Non-Profit Management as an alternative to continue on developing her undergraduate studies. The counselor, covered in cheap perfume, thick glasses and wild curly red hair, started with a series of questions to better understand Audrey's sense of direction.

"Where do you see yourself in five years?" she asked, flipping her hair over her shoulder, her accent from Brooklyn or someplace nearby.

"Oh my gosh, what if I don't know?" She panicked. "I can see myself owning a nonprofit, as a published author or maybe I will still be at the shelter, stuck cleaning out cages, but my mother says it isn't a real job, but I truly believe it is. What if I am all alone? What if my landlord dies and I have to find somewhere else to go? Should I move back home or maybe a different city, but my sister is pregnant and I want to be near the new baby. I am sorry, what was the question?" She nibbled her nails furiously, watching the exhausted expression on the counselors face.

"Let's try a different direction." She let out a sigh. "Is

there anything you have ever felt like you just had to do, like it was burning a hole in ya?"

"Really any of those things…any of it. I have so many dreams that I am unsure where to begin."

"Okay, sweetie. Hate to burst your bubble here," she said and smacked her gum. "I have like one minute until my next appointment. Why don't you take your course books home and spend some time with them. It will come to you and when it does, give me a call."

"When my life's plan comes to me? Are you kidding me? Can't I just enroll and figure it out along the way?" She tried to calm herself.

"You can, but the problem with that is, what if you change your mind halfway through your degree? I am not saying to stall forever, hun. Just give it a couple days to mull it over."

The woman had a point. She needed to slow her roll a little bit. Patient and rash decisions were never her strong suit. A little research on the internet, in the course books and inside her heart should produce the answer within two to three days tops. This would all work out in due time; it had to.

* * * *

The apartment looked perfect. She had really outdone herself with the ambiance. Will would be ecstatic at the amount of effort she had put into making the perfect evening filled with a thousand ways of saying thank you, not to mention she was in desperate need of a thrilling

The Purpose

distraction. The doorbell rang, echoing through the walls. Audrey glanced at herself in the bedazzled mirror by the door, wiping flakes of mascara from her cheeks and smoothing her lipstick. There he stood every ounce of her comfort and much needed friendship wrapped up into the perfect combination of what she had never thought she needed.

"Hey, kid," He pulled Freedom's leash and he came bounding up to the door.

"You brought him!" she exclaimed. "Hi, Freedom!" She ruffled his ears and knelt down to kiss the tip of his nose.

"Um, why are you wearing flannel pajamas?" Will looked her up and down.

"Oh." She cleared her throat. "Your surprise!"

He raised his eyebrows and opened his mouth to question, but she continued, "As a special thank you for sweeping back into my life to save the day and to share with you just how much I miss and cherish the good ole' days, I have recreated my favorite childhood memory of you."

"I'm confused."

"Don't be." She grabbed his arm, pulling him into the apartment. His eyes lit up as he saw the world's largest fort of blankets, couch cushions, curtains and pillows enveloping the whole room. "You see, Will, the greatest memory of my childhood, and more than likely yours, is that night when Mark had you stay over with us because he had a business trip. Do you remember spending like fifteen hours through the night building the biggest fort we possibly could muster?"

The Purpose

"I can't believe this. It is freaking incredible."

She burst with excitement, jumping up and down. "I just really needed a night with my best friend in a fort. Hope that is okay with you," she said and smiled.

He wrapped an arm around her. "It is more than okay."

She disappeared into her bedroom and brought back a set of flannel pajamas with rocket ships on them and tossed them at him. Despite his embarrassment, he agreed and reemerged from the bathroom a few minutes later with his chest hair escaping from the top button and the pant legs mid-calf. Audrey whistled and beckoned him to the tent where he found graham crackers, chocolate, marshmallows and two bottles of merlot.

"Are we making smores? This couldn't get any better." He ripped open one of the chocolate bars.

"Well, I didn't really plan on starting a fire in my living room, so eating them individually will have to do."

They tore through all of the junk food, ordered a pizza, of which Freedom ate a slice and a half, and drank both bottles of wine. Will opened another bottle as Audrey turned up the music and they each performed their version of the robot and mimicked the way Emma and Alex danced; something along the lines of Emma constantly thrusting her hips and Alex tilting side to side like a little teapot. It was exactly like the old days, but this time with alcohol and she couldn't get enough of it. When the energy died down they were found lying flat in the fort, looking up at the glow in the dark stars Audrey had carefully hung hours before.

"Will, can I share something with you?"

The Purpose

"No."

Stop it." She laughed, slapping him with a pillow. "Please, it is really important to me."

"Then why didn't you say so?"

She pulled a small folded piece of paper from the end table in the living room and sat propped up on her pillow like a third grader anxiously awaiting a bedtime story.

"It's a poem." She flushed. "I wrote it."

"Good to see you're writing again, kid."

"Don't laugh and please tell me if it doesn't make an ounce of sense to you."

"Will do. Action!" He pointed his finger at her.

"It is called *The Purpose*.

Where do you find what burns your soul?
How do you deal with what destroys you?
When do you learn to forgive yourself?
When do you start anew?

There is a lost person deep inside,
She is dying to breathe again,
The only trouble is,
She is afraid her heart will never mend.

When a person is beaten,
Torn apart and discarded,
It is only up to them,
To cast aside the regret, and get started.

The Purpose

So, here goes,
Finding her way.
Traveling the path unknown,
Finally having her say.

"That is all I have right now, ridiculous I know." She folded the paper in half and tucked it under her pillow. She looked up to find Will sliding closer to her. Leaning his arm on her pillow and inches away from her face, he said, "You should always write. You are so good at it." Somewhere between the two bottles of wine, the stars in the fort and the comfort of home, the final chip fell and he leaned in and kissed her gently and then again. She breathed him in deeply, smelling all of the best smells, merlot, his cologne, marshmallows and his skin. She never believed in her wildest of dreams that she would want that kiss. Maybe the wine was taking over, but when he pulled away she leaned in for yet another kiss before a word could be spoken.

* * * *

She didn't tell Emma about the kiss, but she did tell Claudia who was beyond overjoyed. "He is soo handsome!" she exclaimed, clearly overjoyed at the idea that Audrey finally had a love interest. Love interest? Who was she kidding? It was Will for goodness sakes. He had only kissed her because he was on his fourth glass of wine and the tent was so romantic. Why had she done that? Why did she set everything up with such a warm feeling to the room? It was supposed to be fun and remind them of their childhood, but

The Purpose

in fact it was the perfect setting for that kiss. She couldn't help but wonder what would become of their friendship. Undeniably, it would make things awkward and unnerving, especially on his side of things.

She had already decided that she didn't want a relationship of any sort, but this is Will we were talking about. They already had a form of the perfect relationship, but did she find him attractive? Sure, he had the softest blue eyes, a chiseled jaw covered in the precisely perfect amount of scruff and the most adorable shortened black curls on top of his head. Sure, he was tall, slender with massive upper arms and the most beautiful hands any man had ever possessed. But it was Will, the man that held the least awkward place in her life. It was amazing having such an uncomplicated friend that she could laugh with and hug without ever worrying about what he was thinking. Time had elapsed, a lot of time since they had last been best friends, but it was like he had never left. Would she need to have the conversation? Let him down gently or would they just pretend like it never happened?

She was heavily distracted with hundreds of questions as she headed to the hospital. She would have to be super careful to avoid the surgical floor where he resided, but there was a distinct chance she would run into him in the cafeteria. They would have to have the conversation eventually, but not today. Today was about making a difference, helping people.

The Women's Center was primarily focused on breast health, screenings, mammograms and things of that nature,

The Purpose

but they also coordinated with the OB for special events and a referral basis. Audrey was designated as a floater to assist with filing, answering phones and making patients feel comfortable. She much more preferred the times when she was able to work with patients throughout the afternoon, learning of their circumstances, fears and inhibitions. The manager of the Women's Center was named Kate and was by far the most likable person Audrey had ever encountered. She laughed constantly and talked furiously with her hands about her upcoming wedding. Standing at a strong five feet two inches, she came up to Audrey's chest and wrapped her arms around her waist at least five times throughout the day. She had spunk and more compassion than she could understand, thus making the patients super comfortable and relieving their fears.

She showed Audrey how to read patients from the time they signed in at the front desk and the best way to comfort their nerves.

"You see Ms. Standall, over there in the corner? When she came in and signed her forms, she tapped the pen feverously and refused to make eye contact. It doesn't take a rocket scientist to understand how scared she is. A quick look in her chart tells me she is battling something fierce and it is best to find a common denominator. Come with me."

Audrey followed the tiny administrator to the coffee machine in the waiting area and started a single brew of French Mocha. As it churned away, sputtering and spitting out a rich, warm scent of grounded beans, Kate threw her head

The Purpose

back in laughter and started stomping her feet like a child.

"Darn me! I am so silly!"

Ms. Standall in the corner looked up from her magazine and immediately lowered her head once more.

"Oh, Audrey, I made this rich French Mocha coffee and I just remembered how much I disliked it last time. It is everyone's favorite around here, but for some reason, I like those sissy coffees. You already had coffee, didn't you?" She shook her head at Audrey, as if encouraging her to say yes.

"I did, thanks though."

"Well, shish! Ms. Standall, would you like my French Mocha?" Kate crouched down next to her seated in the chair, offering the coffee up to her. "We have all sorts of sweet tasting creamers over there." She pointed to the coffee bar.

Ms. Standall nodded and spoke out, "Well, I guess if you girls aren't going to drink it. I suppose it would be okay."

Kate laughed joyfully and handed her the cup. "Ms. Standall, you just made my whole day! Enjoy!"

Audrey watched with adoration as Kate broke down nerve barriers with such a simplistic gesture. It wouldn't cure her cancer, but it certainly would make her more comfortable waiting to see the surgeon. Kate walked back toward her, brunette curls tied in a ribbon bouncing from side to side, right past the coffee machine and back to work.

The Women's Center was a special place, a place that is almost indescribable. It was filled with warm colors of baby

The Purpose

pink and chocolate brown. There were several pictures breast cancer survivors adorning the walls and even collage of women in pink that formed a giant survivor ribbon. The exam rooms were clinical and smelled of antiseptic, but they too were filled with pink flowers, chocolate covered chairs, and set at a low light level option to resist the harsh glow of florescent bulbs.

Audrey spent the rest of the afternoon entering patient information into the electronic record keeping database and calling patients to remind them of their appointments. It was as she was collecting her purse and heading to the cafeteria for bottled water that she noticed a young woman in the waiting area with worn tennis shoes, a jacket with holes in it and the saddest eyes she had ever seen. She was scanning the room nervously as if anticipating everyone's judgment of her, while gently rubbing her left hand up and down on a belly of at least eight months of pregnancy.

Audrey rested her purse on the counter. Deciding against the coffee trick, due to the baby in her belly, she opted instead for conversation.

"When are you due?" She sat down next to her.

"July fourth." She smiled.

"Amazing. My sister is three months along and I am so impatient to meet the little one. I'm Audrey by the way."

"Lacy." She leaned over, stretching her lower back.

"Is there anything you need, Lacy? I am a volunteer here and happy to help in any way."

"I don't really need much, except this surgery to go

The Purpose

...lower on her belly.

"...I ask what type of surgery?" She

...ay. They found a lump in my breast during ...utine check-ups for the baby. I guess I should ... to be pregnant now, because they never would ...noticed it otherwise."

Withholding any panic she felt for Lacy, she reached for her hand instead. "You seem very strong to me, like you can manage anything. Someday this will be such an inspiring story for you to tell the little one."

"Lilly," her face lit up, "I am gonna name her Lilly."

"That is beautiful," she said and smiled back.

Just then, Lacy reached to rub the tears falling from her eyes. It pained Audrey on the deepest level to see someone hurt so badly, regardless if she barely knew her. Even worse, when Lacy wiped the tears from under her right eye, she also wiped away the thick makeup concealing a fist-sized bruise. Audrey blinked twice and then quickly took her gaze back to Lacy's hands. There was absolutely no way any man could beat a woman who was pregnant with breast cancer. How on earth was that even feasible? Her mind ran in a million directions, images of Jason flashing in her head. There was no way she could possibly judge her or try and understand what brought her to this point. She let go of her hand and hugged her tightly.

Surprisingly, Lacy hugged her back and deep sobs escaped her as she leaned into Audrey. Simultaneously, burning tears dripped onto Lacy's shoulder and they both

The Purpose

held each other, sharing a bond that was unspoken but eerily understood. Pulling away from Lacy, she looked her in the eyes. Lacy looked down, embarrassed, suddenly realizing her bruise had been revealed.

"Don't worry," she squeezed her hand again, "I won't tell anyone. Is there anywhere you can go?"

Her sobs were slowing, but equally impactful. "No, I have no one other than him."

Audrey grabbed a pen and paper from the registration desk and wrote down her name, number and address. "I know I don't know you, but believe me when I say I came close once to your exact situation. Everyone needs a friend."

Lacy reached for the piece of paper and folded it gently in her lap. "Why would you do this for me?"

"Women need to take care of each other. Sometimes you just have to have a little faith in people. Call anytime."

With that, she slipped out the door and leaned against the wall, crying just as hard as the day Jason walked out. Something in her stirred, something burned in her soul. This was it, she had to do something. Other women were not as lucky as she and often had nowhere to turn. If she had to do anything in this world, needed to do anything, it was to create a safe place for them to turn to. She couldn't fix the abuse in the world by herself. There was no way she could stop every fist mid-air from coming down on a weak and frail woman, but if there was even the slightest chance she could help them escape, it would certainly help. Not having an inkling of how to make this dream a reality, she suddenly knew the first step in the right direction, her direction for once.

The Purpose

When her tears dried up, she made her way past the gift shop to the cafeteria. The room was bustling with at least a hundred people spilling out into the hallway. All she wanted was a bottle of water and maybe a pack of gum. Rolling her eyes, she turned when a familiar face caught her gaze. He was sitting with Will, tucked in the back corner at the same table she had sat with him the other day desperately pleading for money. They were talking seriously in hushed voices and her father had his hands clamped together in a tight fist. Will sat with his elbows on his knees leaning in toward him with a concerned expression. She walked quickly toward them, her mind racing.

"Dad?" She reached out to touch his arm.

"Bear!" He stood up, guilty.

"What are you doing here?" she insisted.

"Um, just meeting Will here for a bite to eat."

"Dad," she was irritated, "please don't lie to me."

"Audrey," Will started. "Your dad…"

"Don't." She put her hand up. "Dad, why are you here?"

"Oh, bear, this isn't exactly the way I planned on telling you. I have a little bit of cancer I am having removed from my lungs. It is no big deal really, and Will here is making sure they take real good care of me. Don't you worry." He reached for her, but her eyes were filled with tears for the second time that afternoon and she was furious.

"Why wouldn't you tell me? Why would Will know first?" She turned to him with fire flashing in her eyes. "And how could you not tell me?"

The Purpose

Her father reached for her a second time, forcing her into his grasp. He hugged her tightly, letting her cry in the middle of the noisy café. Will put his head down, clearly feeling the lowest he had ever been.

"Now you listen to me, bear, I am gonna have the surgery; they are gonna get it all out and I will be good as new, like a shiny little penny. Don't you go crying all the time and thinking that anything but that is gonna happen to me."

She peered up at his strong, round face. His misty blue eyes were filled with strength and raw emotion. She hugged him again and when she pulled away she looked from Will back to her father. "I believe you; you are going to be fine. I know it," she said, mumbling and once more turning to glare at Will as she hugged him.

* * * *

Her father was admitted two days later, the night before the "Family Fur Fest". Audrey was a wreck in the waiting area, tapping both her feet at the same time nervously. Emma was on her right side with her mother on her left, each flipping through magazines and never reading a thing. Will popped in periodically, offering a familiar face in a dark strange world, but that was all he was able to provide for her. She was devastated that he could hold such a truth that determined a large part of her happiness, her parents. He had tried to talk to her, tried to reason with her, but she was cold as ice. She expected any man in the world to lie to her, to forget what was important, but not Will. The kiss

The Purpose

between them was a distant memory now, as if it were a preview of a romantic comedy she saw in the theater once. The bridge was burned and it was positively irreversible.

Emma didn't even seem to notice the tension between them, nor did she care. Their father was lying on a cold metal table having death ripped from his body right now. Their dear sweet father, always afraid anyone would deprive them of joy, let alone his own problems. He internalized everything, even this. It floored Audrey to imagine a world without him, without the regular phone calls about nothing at all or a holiday without his tearing up because he loved the family just that much.

Her father, and mother too, were beacons of shining hope in a dark rustic world. Without them, she would be so alone. Worse, she had yet to make him proud. He needed to see what she was capable of and meet Emma's baby. She leaned her head in her hands and rocked back and forth, fighting the tears. Will sat beside her and placed his hand on her head, gently rubbing her blonde curls.

Moments later, the surgeon appeared in the waiting area with a huge grin on his face. Clearly pleased with himself, he nodded in their direction. "Mr. Landrow did excellent. We were able to completely remove the cancerous cells without any complications. I anticipate a 100% remission with a little bit of radiation and regular checkups. He is being transported back to his room to rest and let the anesthesia wear off. You will be able to see him shortly." After his grand announcement, Audrey put her head back in her hands and let the tears roll as she thanked God for

The Purpose

giving her more time with her father. Her mother and sister hugged the surgeon and Will bantered back and forth with him in medical terminology and follow-up questions. Audrey didn't care about anything but seeing her father and cherishing every day with him.

At seven o'clock, the following morning, she forced herself out of bed for the biggest day of the shelter's year. "Family Fur Fest" came every year with little to no regard to her personal life. This day was for all of the wet-nosed little pieces of joy that were begging for a home using their only available bargaining chip, their droopy sad eyes. Dressed in her best jeans with glitter on the pockets, a buttoned down pink and purple plaid shirt with metallic buttons, and her hair in a high ponytail, she felt tired but looked exuberant. Her team of volunteers gathered around her by a quarter till eight, ready for direction.

"Thank you from the bottom our hearts for being here today," she yelled out over the crowd. "This day goes on record every year with the most adoptions. Usually we aren't even so lucky to find homes for at least half of the little guys living here. With your help, this year's goal is to find homes for even more and I truly believe we can do it!" The crowd cheered loudly, with a sea of orange volunteer shirts. "Let's get started!"

The next three hours were spent setting up tents, directing vendors and decorating. Banners were hung with photos of select dogs and cats on the front of the building. The country music band, *The Believers*, set-up on the stage in record time with a shiny red drum set and a countless

The Purpose

array of guitars, both acoustic and base. Hay was strewn about throughout the front and backyard, creating a farm-like feel and a local petting zoo arrived with baby cows, pigs, horses and bunnies for holding. Mylar and regular balloons in red, blue, yellow and white covered every inch of the event, including hanging from the clown and stilt-walker's belts. The shelter came alive in color and Audrey stood back from the crowd to admire the best "Fur Fest" yet. It never ceased to amaze her how dedicated her volunteers were.

Once the decorating was complete, the food tent was next with funnel cake machines, cotton candy on sticks and kettle popcorn. A team mixed the lemonade, sweet tea and placed bottled waters in coolers of ice. Old fashioned pieces of wood covered in hand-painted labels directed guests to the restrooms, food and adoption tents.

At exactly twelve noon, families came pouring into the event by the dozen. Previous adopters always brought their dogs, so the grounds were covered in Collies, Labradors, Poodles and every breed imaginable. Children squealed in delight over the petting zoo as parents chased them and their dogs around, clearly exhausted, but amused. The weather was beyond perfect. Not a cloud in the sky could be found and the sun burst through the sky, casting a glow off the band's equipment. It was warm, but not hot and Audrey found herself tying her button-up top around her waist, showing off her bare arms in her white tank top.

An hour into the event, Audrey's mom, sister and Alex showed up for support and Claudia shortly thereafter. Dad

The Purpose

was recovering nicely in his room and insisted they come so he could get some rest. Despite her best efforts, she found herself scanning the crowd for Will, but he was nowhere to be found. She headed up on the stage and tapped the microphone until the crowd gathered and a hush waved over them.

She flashed her greatest smile available and blinked in the sunlight. "Welcome to Family Fur Fest 2012!" The crowd roared, with children jumping up and down and parents whistling and clapping. "My name is Audrey Landrow, and I am the manager here. On behalf of the *Fall in Love Shelter*, I sincerely thank you for joining us today in this amazing cause. Each year, hundreds of animals are dumped on sight without any explanation, or found abandoned or abused. It is a privilege to care for them and connect them to amazing families like you. Without further adieu, let's welcome *The Believers*!" The crowd screeched again. "This rockin' band is going to set the tone for the greatest adoption day ever as we welcome onstage a parade of our most precious dogs and cats available for adoption today. Please, don't hesitate if one of these babies catches your eye. You can take them home tonight!" With that she stepped down the set of stairs to the left of the stage as the band kicked up. Volunteers crossed the stage one by one, holding a huge poster of the animal with its name, age and breed, while another one carried the little pooch or kitten, holding them up on display. The animals never seemed scared; instead they almost knew it was their moment to shine. Audrey stood

The Purpose

to the side, clapping excitedly as she watched the faces in the crowd. It was happening all around her. One by one countless hearts broke in the crowd at the sight of their new best friend.

Squeezing through several dozen people to the lemonade stand, she saw him leaning against the back of the shelter. In blue jeans and a white t-shirt, he had never looked so good. She hated herself for thinking that. She could never forgive him for what he had done. His eyes met hers and she hesitated under the intensity. She couldn't avoid him, just walk away, so she pulled her ponytail tighter and headed in his direction.

"Why did you come here?"

"Come on, Audrey, please don't be like that. I never meant to hurt you."

She studied his eyes, realizing he may be telling the truth, but it didn't undo her loss of trust and faith in him.

"Look, we can't pretend it didn't happen, like you never lied to me. After all I have been through, I would think you would be honest with me about something so important."

Freedom nudged his nose into the palm of her hand with a soft whine as if apologizing for him, while Will's eyes never left hers.

"I trusted you, Will, more than you will ever know."

"You don't get it; it wasn't my story to tell. Your dad was so hesitant because, well I am sure he was scared." His eyes reflected from the sunlight, forcing her to look away. It was like he was looking through her.

The Purpose

"Whatever, Will. You let me down, regardless. You know I would have told you if it were Mark."

She walked away with her stomach sinking lower and lower, until she felt like she was going to throw up. She couldn't help but wonder if she were using this as an excuse, pushing him away so she didn't have to deal with the kiss, or if she was truly mad at him. So many feelings flooded through her: anger, regret and fear. Fear he would go to England and never look back. Even if she wanted her chance with him on a romantic level, wanted to try again at the ever present kiss, something was holding her back. He needed to go away and leave her be with her cynicism and doubts. On a positive note, Freedom had never been happier or healthier.

Will stuck around through the entire event, even after her family had gone. He silently worked alongside the volunteers packing up and taking decorations down. She saw him lifting heavy pieces of the stage to the truck out front and when he caught her eye, time froze if only for an instant. They had adopted out eleven of the sixteen dogs and ten of the cats in the shelter, making this event by far their most successful with sixty percent adoptions and over seventeen thousand dollars raised for the shelter. If only they could host an event of this magnitude a few times a year, they would never reach capacity. However, she seriously doubted any of the major sponsors would support such spending.

When the last piece of hay had been picked up, Audrey watched as Will loaded Freedom into his truck and drove

The Purpose

away into the night. She was heartbroken that he didn't fight for her, didn't even try. Who knew when she would see him again? She finished the evening feeding and locked the shelter behind her. Some time with her father was exactly what she needed.

He was sleeping when she poked her head into his room, sleeping with tubes coming out of so many places. His face was swollen and his eyes were crusted over as if he had been at it for hours. A tray next to his bed held a few magazines, the remote control and two empty containers of orange Jell-O, while the television blared in the background. He looked so peaceful curled up under the blanket that she refused to wake him. Instead, she kissed his forehead and headed home for a bubble bath.

Audrey slept through most of Sunday with August curled at her feet. She woke for a few hours around lunchtime to share a cup of tea with Claudia and cucumber sandwiches. Claudia boasted on her, saying just how proud she was of such a well-organized event and then begged for details about her Ball to come. Audrey refused to give-in to her conniving ways, but promised to take her dress shopping for the big day. She spent the rest of the afternoon drifting in and out of sleep, watching old Frank Sinatra movies and staring at her phone. He never called.

Chapter 9

"I figured it out." She thrust the catalogs of courses back at the red-headed guidance counselor. She peered anxiously through her thick glasses.

"Well?"

"I would like to enroll in the Non-profit Management Master's program; I have a business venture I am seriously considering."

"Care to share?" She seemed far from amused.

"Still working out the details, for now. I just want to get started."

Audrey filled out three forms, enrolled in her first four classes scheduled for the fall. The program would teach her fundraising tactics, organization of a non-profit and how to start one from the ground up. It was ideal, encompassing everything she was ready for. With a little luck, hard work and dedication, her dream was set to come to life. In the meantime, she intended to start writing again. Every step of

The Purpose

her journey should be documented, including her initial "ah-ha" moment at the hospital. This was it, her calling, and she had absolutely no idea how to get started other than listening with an open mind to her professors. If anyone would know the first step she should take it would be them. Not to mention, she was beyond thrilled at the idea of getting back into school. It was the only time that she truly felt herself. The cool crisp autumn air ruffling her hair as she trekked across campus made her feel alive and filled with reason.

Claudia was the first person she wanted to tell for whatever reason. She knocked softly on her door and when she didn't answer the third time, she pulled at the knob to let herself in.

"Claudia? You okay? It is Audrey."

It was silent, other than the soft hum of the record player. She panicked, if only for a minute, realizing that her life would fall apart if anything happened to her newfound friend. She called for her again—nothing. She tiptoed to the back of the dark apartment with only the sunlight casting a beam of light against the hardwood floor. Creaking open the bedroom door, she saw Claudia's outline, lying on her side, facing away from her. *Oh God, please.*

Inch by inch, she made her way to the bed. She didn't hear so much as a breath, and certainly didn't see anything moving. Claudia's hair for once was lying straight on the pillow behind her. Long streaks of black on white woven together, stretched out, making her look so beautiful. Her skin was relaxed and without the normal amount of rouge

The Purpose

and sharp red lipstick. She was natural and so peaceful.

"Claudia?" No response.

She reached for her, slowly. Fingers outstretched, she inched her hand out to her shoulder. Gently, she rocked her arm back and forth. "Claudia?"

"Ahhhhh." Claudia shot out of bed, screaming at the top of her lungs. "What? What's happening?" Her English accent was void.

Audrey jumped back, easily five feet in one bound, heart racing, with eyes bugging out of her head. Claudia panned the room in panic, her eyes finally resting on Audrey.

"Oh Audrey, it is only you." She placed her hands on her heaving chest as if to steady herself.

"Claudia, I am so sorry. I didn't mean to intrude, but when you didn't answer the door I was so scared, and you door was unlocked. Please don't be mad."

Claudia resumed her strong English drawl and smiled immensely. "I could never be mad at you, sweet girl. I was only napping, that's all. If anything I am sorry to have scared you." She tapped the bed, insisting Audrey join her. She hopped up into the California king bed filled with several different feather pillows, silk blankets and Egyptian cotton sheets. She slept like a queen. "What's on your mind?"

As Claudia ran her fingers through Audrey's curls, she recounted the hospital moment with Lacy, her epiphany in the hallway and the visit to the counselor's office. Claudia's eyes lit up with pride and she hugged her with all her

The Purpose

strength. "I am so proud of you, for everything." Audrey was starting to rely on the comfort of her thick accent. There was something about Claudia's opinion of her that validated her every belief. There was no one in the world like her.

* * * *

"It has to be perfect!" Audrey's face was animated and filled with life.

Emma rubbed her belly, which was really starting to show. "Aren't you exhausted from last weekend? I mean, my gosh, bear, you just don't stop."

They were sitting on Emma's large screened in porch in her backyard over looking tall maple trees stretching to the sky. Rocking back in forth in wooden chairs, they sipped sweet tea and let the final spring breezes swarm around them. Summer was on the horizon and that meant Will was leaving. She wanted so badly to tell Emma everything, but for some reason she had a feeling she already knew.

They had always been that way, inseparable. Whatever Audrey was thinking or feeling, Emma felt it too. If Emma fell down and scraped her knee, Audrey wore a bandage also. Whether or not they admitted it or realized it, they were identical in so many ways. They shared the same laugh, nose and hands, each nail with tiny lines running vertically through them, but more importantly they viewed life through the same inspired eyes. They believed in the good in everyone and always chose to forgo their inner doubts to focus on faith alone.

Now, with the sweet chirp of excited new baby birds

The Purpose

testing their wingspan and the sunshine warming their bones, Audrey felt hesitant to connect Emma to the reality. If she spoke the words that were dancing on the tip of her tongue, it would make them real. The last thing she wanted or needed was to accept what happened and hear Emma say Will was right. It was better this way, pushing him out of her life. If he left, maybe when he returned they could go right back to their nitpicking, brother/sister relationship. Emma would scorn her and somehow meddle in the middle, forcing her and Will to work through things. It terrified her and she decided to leave well enough alone until she had the opportunity to figure things out. For the time being, she could only think of the way his skin smelled and the warmth throughout her when he kissed her. *That kiss.*

"So what did you have in mind?" Emma questioned.

"I am thinking string white lights hanging overhead, a solid wood dance floor placed on top of the cobblestone, a cocktail bar in the corner with her signature drink, the dirty martini and everyone dressed to the nines in tuxedos and ball gowns. The music should come from a record player."

"Wow, I am really getting excited, except for the martinis. You couldn't have had this party months ago?" Emma swirled her sweet tea with disappointment.

"Oh stop, all I know is that everyone better be there or I will be so sad for Claudia. She deserves such a special night, a night she will always remember."

"Not trying to be rude here," Emma gleamed her super fake smile, "but what is it about this lady that makes you love her so much?"

The Purpose

"You are rude, all of the time." She smirked. "That aside, she is unique in her own right. Like a character out of a book or fairy godmother of some sort. Age doesn't matter when it comes to friendship and when you spend time with her, you'll understand. Claudia lives in her own majestic and imaginative world and it is fun being a part of it."

"Whatever you say."

"These are going to be a long several months with you this crabby already."

"Yeah, yeah, just deal with it." She threw her straw across the porch at Audrey, missing her by an inch. "You are just lucky to have me."

* * * *

"You are my Everest." Audrey stood at the bottom of the cobblestone hill of her street, staring at the coffee shop near the end. Her eyes were hyper-focused, her determination unyielding. She dressed the part in new black and silver running shoes and a pink iPod strapped to her upper arm with "We are the Champions" by Queen, blasting in her eardrums. There was no way in hell she was going to let this hill get the best of her again. She would become a runner whether her thighs liked it or not. She trotted in place, catching a glimpse of herself in a store's window front. "Yep, kiss this tush goodbye," she yelled out louder than she realized over the music. Taking little notice to the looks of amusement from passersby, she lowered her arms to her ankles in a final stretch.

As the music elevated, she lifted her arms like Rocky

The Purpose

Balboa and took to the streets. She didn't allow herself a slow start, it was all or nothing. She ran as hard as she could breathe to the deepest part of her lungs. She ran for all the times Jason pushed her. She ran for every second she felt scared. She ran because no one was chasing her.

    Chest pumping, heart racing, blonde curls flying, she didn't slow, but ran harder, faster. People and stores whizzed by her in a blurry and furious blaze. She reached out and high-fived the stop sign, but kept on going. Faster, faster until her stride loosened. Her thighs were burning, but felt alive. Her breath steadied and her heart resumed to normal as she reached the perfect speed, a combination of endurance and energy. She was running, running! Past Malian's, past the thrift store at the corner, and on she ran until she could see the wide open river in front, raging with life.

    She jumped across a grassy knoll onto the river's path and continued. She pushed and pushed with new spirit spreading through her limbs. As the wind pushed back against her, splashing her face with clean, sweet smelling air, one by one tears of pride slid across her cheeks. As she ran, her mind raced with every overbearing moment of the last year. She wiped her eyes, looked down at her hands and stopped dead in her tracks. Looking to the sky, she smiled; *forgiveness*.

    A major encumbrance lifted from her life that day. If anyone were watching her cry during that run, they would deem her certifiable insane. It was a moment she had been waiting for, but didn't realize it, not even in the slightest. Every person reaches a point when the suffrage they bear

The Purpose

becomes intolerable. When they finally fight their way out from the pit, they discover a shining light thought to have been long burned out. Life opened up around her and she felt like she could breathe better; everything had a brilliant and pungent smell. She noticed families laughing over spilled ice cream, couples bickering in the park and the way the sun cast a half rainbow over the river.

Nothing in particular happened forcing her to retreat from her crippling sorrow; instead exactly the opposite. It was the simple act of doing something she had always dreamed of, such an empowering moment that would be lost on others. She went for a run and came back a new woman, and if asked, there was absolutely no way she could describe what had just happened. For all she knew, she was losing her mind.

* * * *

"Try this one on, dear." Claudia shook the dress at her giddily.

"Are you sure? That doesn't really look like me in the slightest."

The dress looked musty, like it was from the early 1900s and the thrift store had purchased it under the assumption it must be worth thousands of dollars. That is in fact what they must have believed because the price tag reflected it. It was mustard yellow with a high collar and covered in lace. Each button was different, reflecting the originals had been lost and these were sloppy seconds. However, the pleading look of her newfound friend begged her to try it on.

The Purpose

"Fine."

She came traipsing out of the dressing room, dancing the waltz. Claudia laughed, nodding her head no simultaneously. Audrey smiled in gratitude and went back in the dressing room to strip the ancient artifact from her body. Next came Claudia in a Valentine's Day red floor length gown. It swished when she walked and hugged her perfectly at the waist. Audrey's breath caught in her throat and she had an image of young Claudia with Frank so many years ago. The most beautiful feature of the dress was the way it dipped into a sweetheart shape around her bust line and showcased her softened-with-age arms.

"You are stunning." Audrey clapped her hands together. "Don't you dare walk out of here without that dress."

"You really think so? I feel a little foolish with a strapless. I mean it has been years since these girls have seen the daylight." She jiggled her chest in wonder.

"It makes it all the more appropriate. Show yourself off a little!"

Audrey tried on three more dresses before falling head over heels in love with a black corset dress with silver stitching along each of the hems. It pulled her in tight and pushed everything up that needed to be. The lower half was made of black silk that made her look incredibly sophisticated. Spinning around in the mirror, she understood completely why Claudia always wore ball gowns during the daytime. A woman couldn't possibly feel more beautiful in anything else.

The Purpose

After dress shopping, they made their way down the street to the corner coffee shop and ordered two double espressos and English muffins. Audrey smeared hers in strawberry cream cheese, while Claudia delicately smoothed low fat margarine on hers. The coffee was piping hot, sending swirls of steam up toward her.

"So tell me about this Will." Claudia took a miniature bite of the crispy edged muffin. "I have seen him around quite a bit lately."

"There is nothing to tell."

"Pish," she waved her hand at her, "I may be older than dirt, but don't you dare assume I don't see love when it lands in front of me."

"Love? Ha!" Audrey choked on her coffee, the heat of the espresso burning the roof of her mouth.

"Fine, live your life alone only to wake up on a Sunday morning with only the paper to keep you company. But take a tip from me if you dare." She leaned forward, connecting her vibrant eyes flooded with mascara with Audrey's. It was the same way in which Will had leaned toward her the day he took Freedom home. Audrey shifted in her seat, uncomfortable with the memory.

"I have been watching you, sweet child. I have seen you blossom from a layered bulb buried into the ground on a fall afternoon to the most gorgeous daffodil standing so tall and proud in the garden. You are too hard on yourself, expect too much, and for whatever reason you have convinced yourself that being alone is the only way to make anything of yourself."

The Purpose

Audrey lowered her head, realizing she had never felt so naked and vulnerable. She refused to raise her eyes to meet Claudia's; it was a moment of truth, of shame. She was so concerned with feeling sovereign that she had disregarded anything even remotely close to love, instead marking it hindering, suffocating.

As they drained the last of their coffee before rising to leave, Claudia tried to reason with her once more.

"I am not trying to push you, sweet child."

"I know, really I do." Audrey reached out to hug her. Claudia stroked her hair and whispered into her ear, "I only want you to know that you are capable of real love, and I don't want to see it pass you by."

Together they strolled down the street, arm in arm, with their dresses thrown over their shoulders. It was a good day filled with laughter and beautiful silk dresses, but she couldn't help but wonder about what Claudia had said. She was right and she knew it; then why couldn't she just pick up the phone and call him? There was something holding her back and she hated that about herself. It was as if the world continued moving around her and she once again was at a standstill, refusing to believe in what could be.

Chapter 10

It was better than she imagined it would be. The garden out back was engulfed in twinkling lights of blue and white, gleaming as the sun set. The dance floor was positioned perfectly in the center of the flowers and Alex had managed a disco ball hanging from the Weeping Willow overhead. Audrey had woven additional strands of lights up and around the base of the tree and along the pathway from the door to the dance floor. Alex had assembled a temporary bar in the corner and Emma was currently covering it in lights, as well.

Claudia had begged to see what they were doing on three different occasions throughout the day, but Audrey refused. It was to be a complete and total surprise. With the decorations over and done with, she started in on the music, carefully setting up the record player and stacking the vinyl discs one on top of the other; Frank, of course, and Tony Bennett, Jo Stafford, the Andrews Sisters, Bing Crosby and

The Purpose

Doris Day. She studied the casing to handpick the greatest love songs, along with the ever popular upbeat melodies.

Emma and Audrey had spent several hours that afternoon baking small macaroons, miniature cheesecakes, baby quiches and even bite-sized pieces of sushi. It was eclectic, but divine looking. Alex moved on to mix the liquor, focusing on the drink of the night, the dirty martini, and an assortment of wines and beer. It was quaint and the only thing left to do was get dressed.

She stared at herself in the mirror, trying on different smiles. She was miserable and trying to deny it. Why didn't she just call him? If anything it would have given her the opportunity to see him, if only for one last time before he left. Letting her frown settle in, regardless of her efforts, she focused instead on her makeup. She had carefully selected smoky eye shadows of grey, silver, black and a glittery white shade appropriately named "star". Layer by layer, she built her look from the array of colors, finally sweeping liquid eye liner across her lids and generously applying mascara from the inside of her lashes outward. Her mother had always taught her to highlight one feature alone on her face when it came to makeup, so tonight it would be her eyes. She had been blessed with long, full eyelashes, so it was always her first choice.

Aside from her eye makeup, she also selected a glimmering bronzer to bring her tired face to life and a pale nude lipstick to complete the look. She swept her hair into a curly up do with select pieces falling near her face, and slipped her dress on. She couldn't help but smile at herself

The Purpose

in the mirror when all was said and done. For once, in a long time, she felt beautiful. Even if there was no one there to truly appreciate her efforts, it sure felt nice.

Emma was finishing changing, having purposely selected a gown that hugged her midsection. She had always been very tiny, but there was nothing more beautiful than her little baby bump pushing out from under her dress. When she finally emerged, her face sagged with frustration. "I look fat." She tightened her fist, forcing a vein to show on her forehead.

"Oh come on, why do pregnant women always say that?" Audrey rolled her eyes while she tightened two bobby pins holding her hair together.

"Because it's true! People look at me with the sideways glance, wondering, is she pregnant, or is she fat? That is why I rub my belly! It is the tell tale sign that there is something more to this than eating too many cheeseburgers and fries!" She tugged and pulled her dress out away from her belly, causing it to stretch and then bounce right back to her skin. "Hopeless."

Alex snuck up behind her and wrapped his arms around her, kissing her neck. "God, you're gorgeous! Who is the lucky guy who gets to take you two home tonight?"

"Ugh." Emma flung his hands from her and marched off down the stairs and out back to the garden. Alex barely noticed. "Get it? You two, meaning her and little Luke?"

Audrey's jaw dropped. "You know it is a boy?"

"Oh, she didn't tell you?" Instead of sticking around to own up to the secret he just told, he took off running after

The Purpose

Emma, leaving Audrey alone with her tears welling up. She was seconds behind him, finding Emma still adjusting her dress with a look of exasperation.

"It's a boy?" Audrey reached for her and held on tight. "Why didn't you tell me?"

"I am going to kill him! Alex can't keep a secret to save his life." Emma turned to reciprocate the hug. "We wanted to wait until later tonight, when Mom and Dad are here."

"Dad is going to be floored to know that you are naming him after him." A little sadness filled her. She was missing these special moments in life. If only she had never met Jason, maybe she would have met someone else and would be getting married or the one struggling with her pregnancy weight. She quickly negated the thoughts, forcing herself to be filled with only pure happiness for Emma right now. Emma, Alex and little Luke.

One by one, the party came to life. The first to arrive were, in fact, Audrey and Emma's parents. Her father looked dynamite in his tuxedo. He laughed his hearty laugh, saying this was his "big debut". Finally feeling well enough, he was able to leave the house behind and smell the fresh night air. He was only able to stand for about ten minutes at a time, but he looked wonderful. His face was filled with color once more and his eyes were enamored with the strength of life and second chances.

Audrey's mother was adorned with a long gold dress with a halter strap. It was elegant and fit for a queen. It had been far too long since everyone had the opportunity to play dress up. She strutted around "oohing" and "ahhing" at how beautiful

The Purpose

everything was, saying her girls had done such a splendid job.

Next to arrive were Audrey's two boisterous aunts and uncles from her father's side. She had insisted they come due to the sheer fact that they were the life of the party, regardless of where they went. It was a guarantee that they would get along seamlessly with Claudia, as well. Mark knocked over a potted plant on his way in the door, chuckling at himself and running for Emma and Audrey. There was never any mention by Emma of Mark coming, but she assumed maybe her parents had told him. A small glimmer of hope shot through Audrey's heart at the idea of him telling Will about the party.

A half hour into the "Ball" the final guests arrived; two of the volunteers from the shelter, Zach and Britney. She had known them for over fifteen years, previously as classmates and now as beloved friends. They, too, were dressed for the occasion with a ball gown and tuxedo in tow. Audrey hushed everyone down and snuck off to find Claudia for her grand reveal.

She found her attempting to sit patiently on her lavender felt couch with nerves of steel.

"Knock, knock," she said and slipped into her apartment. "We are *finally* ready for you." She threw her hands up with exaggeration.

"What, oh." Her face was tired and worn down, as she slumped over onto the armrest.

"Hey you." Audrey sat next to her, adjusting her skirt. "Everything okay?" She continued to study Claudia's face. Something wasn't right.

The Purpose

"Fine," she muttered, studying her hands and running her fingers over the indented lines.

Audrey sat quietly, waiting for her to make the next move. For some reason, she felt she shouldn't rush her, shouldn't push her beyond her comfort zone. She leaned her head on her shoulder and heard her breathing, shallow and faint. Finally, she spoke, softly, "I shouldn't go."

"Why?" Her heart dropped, confusion and fear racing through her mind.

"I look atrocious and everyone will laugh." Her eyes closed and she leaned her head against the back of the couch. Audrey quietly reached for her hand. She was timeless, ageless, and this was not like her in the least.

"I do believe my age of glamour has passed." Claudia continued speaking with short, ragged breaths, while her eyes remained closed.

"Claud, what changed? You were so excited earlier."

When she didn't respond, she slipped into the kitchen to get her a glass of water. She returned to find her eyes still closed. She was resting now, best not to wake her. She slid out the door, quietly leaving her be. Back downstairs, she politely explained Claudia had a horrendous headache and she would be down in a bit. Her heart felt so heavy. She didn't want to tell anyone, didn't want to embarrass her. She was so beautiful in her dress. No one could ever tell by looking at her what was lurking underneath.

She continued on with the party, serving sweet treats and filling her guests with cocktails. She watched the clock out of the corner of her eyes and found herself cleaning

The Purpose

aggressively. Where was he when she needed him? Why didn't he come? She felt her eyes water, realizing she was finally admitting to herself that she needed him. She needed someone that could help her through life's little insignificant, yet oddly important moments. She slammed the metal ice container closed in a furious rage.

"Sweet bear, why are you slamming things?" Her dad reached for a mini broccoli and cheese quiche without ever taking his eyes off her. "You did a hell of a job on this party, by the way."

"Thanks, Dad," she said and sighed. "Now that you're better though, I get to be mad at you for not telling me."

She couldn't see from the other side of the bar, but he was bracing himself for support. He still felt incredibly winded, even from talking for only a moment.

"Now, that just isn't right. You know better than to think you can be mad at me."

She smiled. "Dad, Claudia is refusing to come down. She seems to think this whole thing is…" Before she could even get the words out, the sweet sound of an English accent was music to her ears.

"Darlings, how sweet of you to come to our little affair!"

Audrey spun around and broke out into laughter with great relief. It was silly, the whole idea of a mad English woman from downstairs needing everyone to wear ball gowns and tuxedos. Yet, everyone at the party embraced it, maybe even realizing that a corny night with great friends was reassuring in a rugged world. This celebration of all

The Purpose

things important was picturesque.

Claudia reached for her and hugged her tightly. All of the guests cheered loudly with her entrance as she strutted around embracing everyone. Audrey watched in awe as the woman who was utterly broken moments ago could fill the room with life and energy once more. She was the kind of person that people were drawn to. It was impossible not to love her. One by one she squeezed cheeks, pinched behinds and twirled around in her lovely gown. When she reached for the last person in the group, Audrey gasped and felt Emma slip her arm through hers.

"You always seem to think you can sneak one by me."

"How did you…"

"I know everything," Emma proclaimed proudly. "The sooner you realize you love him, and tell him that, the sooner your life can begin."

"You are out of your mind." Audrey lowered her gaze, shifting her eyes instead to her father who was staring right at her, staring at Will. Great, now everyone knew.

"What are you so afraid of? He is nothing like Jason. It is our Will. We grew up loving and trusting him. In some way, I do believe we all knew you two would end up together. Audrey, don't let him go to England. Tonight is your chance."

Emma walked away, leaving Audrey paralyzed. It was out in the open. The idea of her loving Will floated through the crowd and played on the lips of those who knew her best. Will couldn't possibly know how she felt; she had done everything to keep him from her.

The Purpose

He looked bewildered by Claudia as she made him turn around so she could have a better look at his behind. Audrey laughed out loud as Will started to perspire and Claudia nodded in approval. When she finally released him from her grasp, he headed toward her. She tried to busy herself with the dirty glasses and possibly avoid the conversation all together, yet she was secretly thrilled at whatever he possibly had to say. He was gorgeous, in a Dean Martin mixed with George Clooney kind of way. He wore a black suit with a tie, thin and not overbearing. His shoes were shiny and his hair relatively maintained, which had always been a challenge for him. The most impressive part of his whole appearance was the fact that his signature facial scruff had been erased and replaced with a smooth, tan jaw line. He was breathtaking.

"Can we talk?"

She dropped a martini glass, forcing everyone to stop and turn toward her. In the silence, she was sure she heard Emma laughing. She struggled to scoop up the pieces and he bent down next to her to help. Silently, they worked alongside one another, breathing the same air, him inhaling her intoxicating floral perfume and her resisting his rustic after-shave.

"We have to talk; we can't go on like this forever."

She turned toward him, finally allowing herself to make eye contact. A pain shot through her chest; this could possibly be the last time they spoke for over a year. Why couldn't she just say what she was feeling? If he rejected her, at least he would be out of the country until she had

The Purpose

time to recover. Not to mention, if he did reject her she would be free and clear to continue on with her simple life. She was prideful in the way things were going; they wouldn't have to change. Besides, how on earth would they ever make a long distance relationship work for that long?

"Will, it is good to see you. We are okay; everything is all right."

He studied her curiously. He watched as she blinked rapidly, which she always did when she was nervous. Next would come her chewing on her fingers.

"What changed?" His voice was steady, forceful.

She looked at everyone in the room, except him. Pulling her pointer finger to her mouth, she was shocked when he grabbed her arm. "What are you doing?"

"Why are you nervous? It is just me. Tell me what changed."

"Will, I guess I just overreacted. I get why you respected my dad's wishes, but it scared me, like I couldn't trust you. He is okay now, so I am over it. Can we just have a good time please? I have had more than my share of drama tonight."

"You are strange. Whatever, if that is what you want." He continued studying her, waiting for her to smile, laugh or get pissed off. She was numb, expressionless and it disturbed him. She walked quickly away, as if she had somewhere important to be, so he was disappointed to see that she only headed over to fix a strand of white lights near the entrance. It was her getaway excuse; she needed to get away from him.

She couldn't understand what was wrong with her. She was dying inside for him to show up and when he did, she couldn't get away fast enough. He could see through her. He would know if she were lying or hiding something, so she felt it best to avoid him. She felt his eyes on her, watching her every step. That was the problem with growing up with someone; they always knew what you were thinking and what every expression meant. He was as close to her as Emma and could easily figure out if she were nervous or scared.

Emma slipped across the dance floor out of Alex's arms and into Audrey's face.

"What happened? Did you tell him? What did he say?"

Even pregnant, she still had more energy than anyone she had ever known. She was bouncing up and down, eyes wide with excitement.

"Nothing, calm down. You are making that baby bounce."

"Tell me!" She gripped Audrey's arms, leaving white marks from her fingers.

"Wow. Okay, so here it is. I told him I wasn't mad at him anymore."

"And?"

"That's it. Said we were fine and that we just needed to have a good time, no drama."

"I can't believe you. Well, the night isn't over and if you don't tell him, then I will."

"All right, stop it! I don't know what I am feeling and you are just complicating things. Leave it be, Emma."

The Purpose

Emma shot daggers with her eyes, looking feistier than ever. "You are a pain in my ass." She stomped off across the party to Alex, definitely involving him in some way.

The evening carried on without a hitch. Claudia was no doubt the bell of the Ball. She danced with everyone, including the women, forcing them to spin and twirl like they were on Broadway. Her laughter could be heard miles above the small crowd and it was contagious. When she laughed, so did everyone around her. Audrey slammed a dirty martini and gained the courage to join her on the dance floor. Before she knew it, she was letting loose and laughing so badly her sides hurt. Mark was doing some sort of Irish jig, while her mother was slipping off her shoes preparing to start the conga line. It was a true success and the only thing plaguing her was the solemn look from Will across the party.

He couldn't be happy, no matter how hard he tried. He was furious with her. She pretended like nothing had happened, after the only real fight they had ever had. Sure, he shouldn't have lied to her, but this was different. Her father was as close to his as possible and there was no way he would ever disrespect him. He thought they could slip away from the crowd for a few minutes and he could tell her why he had done those things. He was only trying to protect her and her family. She was dancing wildly now, obviously one too many cocktails in and pretending not to notice him.

When the music died down, Claudia was found near the record player quieting the crowd. She fashioned a small stage out of the back porch step and stood perched on her tippy toes, martini in hand.

The Purpose

"My darlings, there is only one person I have ever truly loved in my life."

The group gathered and when it was perfectly silent, so silent the crickets could be heard in the background, she snapped her fingers at Mark, who held the record in his hand. He slid it onto the player and lowered the handle.

"The only person I have ever loved…" She paused, batting her eyelashes. "Gene Austin!"

Everyone looked at each other, sideways glances. Clearly, he was way before their time. They were quieted once more, as her sweet voice lifted over the crowd singing. "Just a turn to the right, you find a little white light. It will lead to my, little blue heaven. You see a smiling face, a fireplace, a cozy room. A little nest nestled where the roses bloom. Just Molly and me, and a baby makes three. We're happy in my little blue heaven."

"My Blue Heaven", apparently the most calming and peaceful song ever written. Audrey didn't know the words, but she swayed with the sound of Claudia's belting voice. She sang so wonderfully. It came from somewhere deep down inside her, as if she had been waiting for years to sing that song. It filled everyone with romance and it was as close to any Heaven Audrey had ever known, other than her pond out back of her parents' house. One by one, she noticed the couples in the crowd break off into pairs as they swayed back and forth to her voice. When the final note was sung, she dipped in a perfectly planned curtsey and refilled her martini glass shooting a wink in Audrey's direction. *Who was this woman?*

The Purpose

As everyone carried on, Emma too slipped from the crowd. She made sure Audrey wasn't looking as she tiptoed around the record player and lifted a special record from her bag. She had to order it on eBay, because apparently no one sells records anymore. Twenty dollars and two weeks later, it had finally arrived, offering promise of one last chance between Audrey and Will. If she couldn't do it herself, then Emma would just have to help. As she lined up the needle perfectly, the music floated through the night.

She watched Audrey's face, waiting for the song to sink in. Boy, did it sink in. Her face flushed red and her eyes scanned the room until she saw Emma smiling sneakily, finger still on the needle. She stepped back from the crowd, trying to breathe. Where was he? Did he realize what song this was? She thought seriously for one minute about rushing the record player and flinging it into the flower beds, but Emma would definitely give a struggle and she was pregnant, so she could offer very little defense.

She bit her nails one by one, anxiously waiting. She didn't know what she waiting for, but the song kept getting louder and louder. Was she turning the volume up? Suddenly, she felt a warm hand on hers pulling it from her lips. "Audrey…Landrow…ask…me…to…dance."

Will propped his arm up on her shoulder, leaning into her, mocking the way she had once forced him to dance with her. He was laughing, laughing! It wasn't so serious anymore and they took to the dance floor. They were the only two out there and Claudia, Emma, Alex and her parents watched, transfixed. They started out slow, easing into the

The Purpose

music. When the beat picked up they broke out in their moves they had practiced at her apartment, Will mocking Alex and Audrey poking fun at Emma. They instantly knew what was going on and tried to act offended, Emma screaming out over the music, "We are good dancers!"

Audrey laughed the same hearty laugh of her father as Will dipped her so low her curls grazed the cobblestone. When he pulled her to him once more, she inhaled deeply catching her breath in the back of her throat. He held her close, swayed side to side and when the music finally ended, he spun her away from him and let her go into the crowd. She whirled away, the family and friends spinning around her and landed in her father's arms, who instantly kissed her forehead. Everyone started clapping and Will took a bow.

Unsure of what had just happened; she leaned against her father for a moment to steady herself. They were back, their friendship was alive and well and she couldn't help but wonder if that was all he really wanted. After all, he gave her that grand speech about not dating Blake, claiming she wasn't ready to be with anyone yet, that she needed some time to herself. Then why had he kissed her? She wasn't sure whether she was spinning from the dance, the overwhelming emotions or the martinis, but she excused herself and headed inside.

She collapsed on her bed, the room spinning. August jumped on top of her and tucked himself neatly under her arm. He always had the magic touch. She laid in the darkness thinking of all of the times she had spent with Will. There were hours upon hours shared working in their clubhouse.

The Purpose

They had attempted starting a town newspaper, building a rocket ship, planting vegetables in the garden and selling them on the side of the road. They once spent an entire day creating different cookies and offering samples to her mother, who politely smiled, although they were made of lunchmeat, Goldfish Crackers, pretzels and even popcorn. He taught her how to ride her bike, swing and even learned how to braid her hair when her left arm was broken. They were inseparable and believed that their friendship would last a lifetime. Maybe it would, maybe this is all it would ever be.

She heard her door creak open slightly and saw only his curls in the gleam of the light. He tiptoed toward her and squatted down to eye level. He smoothed her hair out of her face and gently called out her name. She wanted to sit-up and latch onto him, tell him everything she was feeling inside, but she felt paralyzed. It was as if her entire body was strapped down to the bed and her mouth muffled by duct tape. She lay, like a wounded deer in the headlights, her mind tortured with everything she wanted to say and absolutely no concept of how to make herself irresistible. She wanted him to kiss her, wanted him to lean in and just envelop her into the world's most perfect kiss. She waited. He waited.

He leaned in, rubbed her cheek with his softened hand and when she didn't stir, he planted an almost unnoticeable, yet somewhat sweet peck on her forehead. She saw him walking out, one foot in front of the other. He was leaving; he didn't want to wake her. She saw his hand slide the door closed behind him and instead of screaming out, begging

The Purpose

him to stay, she closed her eyes, feeling every tear verging on the edge of an even greater sadness. Last winter, she was alone, crying on the floor, watching Jason walk out and leave her alone, seeing his footsteps, one in front of the other. He left her to cry for days, never once checking on her. She had thought her life was over, having become so accustomed to his abuse. Now, she lay watching the closest thing to real love she had ever known leave in the exact same fashion. She curled into an even tighter ball and sobbed. *He left her*. Once more, she pulled August close and cried herself into a deep, somber sleep. If God were listening, he would let her sleep until next year when Will came home.

Chapter 11

She woke to Emma banging around in the kitchen and Alex whistling some sort of cartoon theme song. Her head was splitting and she had yet to figure out why they were still in her house. She slouched into the kitchen, still in her dress from the prior evening and hair thrown every which way.

Alex whistled. "Well, my aren't we pretty!"

"Shut up. Shut up! What the hell is going on out here?"

Emma smacked a wooden spoon against a metal saucepan and yelled out, "Wake up, princess! I need to know details. Did you kiss him? Did you do more than that? We had no idea where you went off to, but I had a sneaking suspicion."

"Ugh." She slumped down onto her couch and pulled her teal throw across her bare legs. "Did you guys unplug everything and bring in the record player?"

Alex laughed. "Well someone had to! You, your parents, that mad Claudia lady all went in various drunken directions simultaneously and me and Preggo had to clean up the mess, no offense, Mama." He flashed a grin in Emma's direction.

"Thanks," she muttered.

The sun was so very bright, peering through the bay window. No doubt, every other guest from the party was still sleeping at this hour, except for her.

"Well," Emma pressed. "What happened? I am dying here."

"Nothing, I think he left when I was sleeping."

"You're lying."

"No, I am not. I was lying in bed and I thought I heard someone come in. Might've been him, not sure."

"You are lying! Your eye twitches when you lie; you pretended to be asleep so you wouldn't have to talk to him! You cried your little self to sleep because you have mascara all over your entire face. Why in the hell would you do that?" Emma's voice was piercing now.

"Fine, whatever. I just didn't want to deal with it. I don't think he feels the same way."

"Sorry, you don't think he feels the same way? Where were you when he was spinning you around to 'Can you feel the love tonight?' You're welcome by the way. He couldn't keep his eyes off you and if Alex ever held me that close, I wouldn't ever leave him, no offence, love."

"Thanks," he muttered.

The Purpose

"It was just a dance. Besides, I am sure he is leaving soon. Maybe he will come by to talk today, or something."

"Oh, Audrey, he won't." Emma crossed the room and lifted Audrey's hair from the chair. Her voice softened. "His flight left this morning at seven."

Chapter 12

Summer

The heat was unbearable. The sun pushed down on her, burning her shoulders, making her sweaty hair cling to her neck. The newest member of their family, "Berry" the Greyhound, was taking her sweet time frolicking in the back field behind the shelter. She gave her a gentle tug on her collar, attempting to bring her back to reality. "Hurry up, Berry, it is too hot out here to be taking this much time!"

She didn't hurry, if anything, newly excitedly, she sniffed various blades of grass as if they were smothered in dog food. As she sweltered in the sunshine, Audrey was reminded of the lack of it in Will's life. England must surely be cooler and even presenting rain to the thirsty flowers and trees. He consumed her thoughts, every moment of every day. If only he had left Freedom with her instead of his dad, she could have had a small piece of him, at least.

The Purpose

It was impossible to think of anything other than what he was doing at precisely that moment. On countless occasions, she forced thoughts out of her head of him and precious little English nurse falling madly in love. She had her named and exactly described in her head, so clear to her that she could have written a character description in a book.

Her eyes were hazel, the kind that reflected bits of green and gold in them. Her hair would be long and blonde, just like Audrey's, and she would have a little space between her teeth that was so minute it made her even more beautiful. She spoke so eloquently with her accent, that Will was constantly entranced. Freckles poised perfectly on her rosy cheeks left her looking like a celebrity and the girl next store all at the same time. They would go for walks on lunch; maybe she could show him around town. One night they would have one too many glasses of wine and he would confess how uncomfortable his fully furnished flat was and she would offer so innocently for him to stay with her for the evening. If anything to make the morning commute to the hospital easier, or because she absolutely insisted that they have a fresh espresso as the morning broke through. They would laugh through the night, just as he and Audrey had, making his mind drift to her if only for a second until the gorgeous little English nurse would tell him something funny that was so absurd it would eliminate all memories of the poor, childhood friend who was so lost that no one could save her.

When he eventually returned home, she would be on his

The Purpose

arm, enchanting everyone in his life, including Audrey, and then they would return to England to continue their medical practice together in a cottage near the city. Audrey would fall from his radar as a girl he once knew and she would spend the rest of her life hopeless and alone, drowning in the memories of Jason's hurtful words and the image of Will's fingers pulling the door closed behind him.

These thoughts alone kept her dismayed and void of all real hope. Her financial situation couldn't exactly afford her a trip to England to confess what she forgot to mention in the states before he left, but even if they could she would have no idea what to say when she ran into him and his gap-toothed marriage material. The whole situation was impossible and school was starting soon anyway. She would do what she had always done growing up and that was to pour herself into books, education and the immortal lives of characters in books. Even if her life couldn't end well, theirs always did and could she not dream just a little within the lines?

Alex and Emma were right; she had completely missed her chance. He was gone and more than likely moving on. All of the efforts she had put into improving her life and getting over Jason were destroyed the day Will left. It was as if she were starting from square one. Nothing tasted good anymore, she slept all of the time and while she was running almost four days a week before, she was only down to one now. The shelter was quiet, Emma and Alex were vacationing in Maine with his parents and even the writing that she had begun was mocking her from her computer. She

The Purpose

was alone, confused and so very sad. August watched on as she cried herself to sleep, only then to find relief in dreams filled with memories of Will. She had tried calling him, only once. The connection didn't complete, more than likely because of the distance, but she took it as a sign.

To make all matters worse, she found herself in the midst of the worst cold she had ever had. Cold was in the loosest sense of the word. Her nose was permanently filled with the world's greatest version of disgusting and she could not stop sneezing. Tissues covered her apartment and her office at work and this pathetic version of her life had continued for the last week and was unrelenting. Claudia had offered solitude by making chicken noodle soup and looked heartbroken when Audrey politely refused. She had told her at least fifteen times since they had known each other that she didn't eat meat, broth or anything with a mother.

Claudia shouldn't be discounted though, for she was the only saving grace in Audrey's life at all anymore. They went for dozens of walks in the garden and to the coffee shop. She had introduced her to fantastic black and white movies, such as *Some Like it Hot,* with Marilyn Monroe as Sugar. She was glamorous, irresistible, attainable, cute and sexy all at the same time. Claudia spoke the movie lines out loud simultaneously as Marilyn, "Story of my life. I always get the fuzzy end of the lollipop." They crammed bags of popcorn, boxes of chocolate and bottles of champagne down their throats, which for Claudia was living at its finest and the only way to numb the pain for Audrey.

Aside from sulking through the day alongside Audrey,

she had also convinced her to try a few new things. She set her up with a pastor from a local church, claiming religion was the only way to pull her out of her funk. Audrey complied, recounting the hours of prayer she had pursued recently. He was a tall man with a toupee much darker than his regular hair. He was very serious, so serious, in fact, that Audrey felt nervous sharing her story with him. She instead chalked it up to complication in her love life, insisting that it would pass with time. He loaded her down with passages from the Bible and told her to come back when she was finished. She followed every word of his advice, knowing he was brilliant in his own right and spiritual healing was precisely what she needed. She had even started attending the church with Claudia and grazing through stories of biblical inspirations on Sunday. Although this newfound persistence of religion was helping, and she was increasingly growing closer to her faith, she still felt miserable.

"Darling, talk to me. Why won't you just call the boy?" Claudia was over for their Sunday Bible study, which almost always turned into a gossip fest.

"Oh Claudia, it isn't that simple. He made his choice and I made mine. Besides, this is what I wanted. I wanted some time to myself. Life shouldn't revolve around men. I can be happy without him." Audrey closed her Bible, instead reaching for one of Claudia's cinnamon muffins, still warm from the oven.

"You know something; it is perfectly acceptable to admit that you need a man. But let me clarify by saying that it is only when it is the right man that you feel that nagging sense of need for them. A woman can pursue every ounce of adventure, joy and freedom independently, but when it comes to true love, you will never feel that hole in the pit of your stomach go away until you at least try."

"I just need more time. I need to start school and get my head on straight before I go chasing after someone that may not even feel the same way."

The phone startled her and she made her way over to the couch to pick up her cell.

"Hello?"

"Hi." The female voice was quiet, nervous. "Is this Audrey?"

"It is. Who is this?"

"You may not remember me, but a month or so back, you gave me your number. My name is Lacy."

The image of Lacy's tear-stricken face came to mind. "Of course, I remember you. How could I forget? How are you doing?" She didn't want to push, but something in her gut was telling her this girl needed help.

"I'm...okay, I guess. I am actually in the hospital right now. I delivered Lilly last night."

"Wow! Congratulations! Are you feeling all right, everything good with Lilly?"

"Yes, we are doing fine, thank you. The reason I am calling," her voice lowered, almost to a whisper, "is there any way you can come see me? You know, talk in person?"

"Just name it," she said, trying to sound reassuring and supportive. "I will be there."

The Purpose

* * * *

She entered the hospital halls that had become oddly comforting to her. It took everything to keep her from crying at the thought, or more so the wish, of Will's curly hair appearing around the corner. Every man in a pair of blue surgical scrubs jolted her heartstrings a bit, but she forged on to the OB unit. She had only volunteered a handful of times since Will left. It was too hard.

She carried a pink stuffed bunny and a bouquet of lilies for Mom. She had already decided whatever she needed, or asked, she would do anything she could to help her. This could have easily been her in this hospital room, holding Jason's baby a year ago. It was only by a miracle that she made her way out of that situation. She cringed at the idea of him yelling, "I will beat that baby out of you if you ever get pregnant." He was and always would be a right triangle, expecting only a congruent, compliant match. Any other attempt was seen as failure in his eyes.

The sun was setting and the baby suites had oversized panel windows that looked over an open field. A warm radiance was shining into Lacy's room and she was found curled over on her side with one arm stroking Lilly's face in her little plastic tub next to the bed. Audrey paused for a moment. This was the most beautiful sight; a mother with her newborn infant was quite possibly the most amazing thing in the world. They were so peaceful and she heard Lacy singing softly as Lilly's eyes remained tightly closed. She was bundled in a pink blanket, hand-woven with real

The Purpose

yarn. On her little head sat a matching pink beanie hat that boasted a small ball of yarn on top. She was only six and half pounds, by far the smallest baby Audrey had ever seen. She was breathtaking, rosy cheeks and pouty little lips gently sucking at the air. The tiniest hand in all of history was outstretched on top of the blanket.

"Hey pretty ladies." Audrey knocked gently to not wake Lilly. Lacy turned and tears immediately brimmed over as she reached for her. Audrey squeezed Lacy as much as her small frame would allow. She wanted so badly to lift all of the pain from her and take it on as her own. Lacy eventually pulled back, wiping the tears from her swollen face. She had to be only around twenty years of age, barely an adult, with long, straight brown hair that was presently twisted into a braid.

"How are you feeling?"

"Pretty miserable. I had to have a C-Section and a mastectomy all at the same time. They claim they got it all, but I feel so lost without my breast. They told me I am the youngest woman that has ever had breast cancer in this hospital. I just can't believe that this has happened to me." Silent tears rolled, one after another, down her cheeks to her bright pink hooded sweatshirt. "I just feel so alone, you know?" She wiped her nose with her sleeve.

Audrey was trying so hard to be brave, seeing so much of herself in Lacy's eyes. "You are not alone, you're not. Whatever you need, we are friends now."

"God must have sent you. That is the only thing I keep telling myself. No one I have ever met has been as nice as

The Purpose

you have." Her voice had a southern tint to it, making her even sweeter than what met the eye.

"Well, little Lacy, I have all the time in the world, so why don't you fill me in and then I have one favor before I go. I absolutely have to hold Lilly for only a moment."

Lacy laughed through her tears, more than likely for the first time in months. "She is the only good thing I have done with my life, that is for sure." She took a few short breaths and then slid off the bed into the chair next to it, while Audrey settled onto the window seat.

"My parents died two years ago and I have been on my own ever since. I met this guy and he kind of took me in because I didn't have any money to pay for my parent's house, so I lost it. He hit me a few times in the beginning, but he was always so sorry. He promised it would stop. If I ever had anywhere to go, I would have left, but I have been working as a waitress, trying to save up enough money for college."

She paused to take a drink out of her oversized jug of water and to adjust Lilly's blanket.

"Long story short, I have been living in hell for the last year or so. I got pregnant with Lilly, found out I had cancer, and have been trying to plot my getaway, but there have been so many medical bills that I haven't been able to save much."

Audrey reached for her hand. "Does he know where you are now?"

"No, that is the only thing I have going for me. I packed as many of my things as I could and figured I would ask someone here at the hospital if they knew somewhere I could go, and then I remembered you and how kind you were. I really don't want to lose her." She covered her face as heavy sobs rocked her shoulders once more. This poor woman was completely alone and terrified, woman in the loosest sense of the word, more like strong young girl.

She continued on with stories of the prior months, the multiple threats if she ever tried to leave and the fear she still lived with. She shared the gory details of how they found cancer and her fear of losing Lilly all together. Audrey listened patiently, nodding when appropriate and crying when she couldn't control it. At one point, her mouth opened, words escaped her, and not knowing where they came from, she embraced her outward decision.

"You will come home with me, you and Lilly. You are not alone; you have me." Lacy's expression relayed what Audrey was feeling. This idea was ludicrous. If they were successful in hiding from the potentially dangerous father, they would struggle with figuring out a living situation in a small townhouse apartment with a newborn baby to care for. They didn't even know each other; two women from heartbreaking pasts trying to navigate free will in a foreign friendship.

"I couldn't possibly, you don't even know me. I was only hoping you could help me find a shelter or somewhere to go. I could really use a friend right now, that's all."

The sincerity in her eyes was strong. It was obvious she felt helpless, but refused to take advantage of anyone. It seemed to kill her to ask for even guidance, but it wasn't about her anymore.

The Purpose

"May I?" Lacy nodded, and Audrey reached in and scooped Lilly into her arms. She sighed gently and then stretched her little legs shakily. All the light in the world was wrapped in this fuzzy pink blanket. This is where it all started, the crazy journey of life. Each of us, even the horrible people, started out this dependent and hopeful. No one would get near this little angel if she had anything to do with it. She rocked her back and forth, watching as her eyes fluttered. One could only imagine her little dreams.

"You don't have a choice anymore, everything is about her." Audrey shifted her gaze to meet Lacy's. "You can stay with me until you get on your feet. I even have a job in mind for you. We will start there."

Hesitant and nervous, Lacy clearly struggled with the demand. If life had presented any other opportunity, she would have denied it, but there was something about Audrey. She was almost like family immediately. She smiled constantly and had the largest, most earnest eyes of anyone she had ever met. Without any further questions, she whole heartedly agreed. She smiled, suddenly having a very good feeling about all of this.

Lacy was in the hospital for an additional seven days due to her mastectomy. Audrey visited constantly and even took the liberty to bring her favorite books, magazines, and even her iPod for her to listen to. The talked rapidly, sometimes over the other, making honest attempts to get to know each other. The room was filled with laughter and Audrey found herself quickly falling in love with Lilly. For once, since Will had left she found joy in each day. In the

The Purpose

evenings, she worked tirelessly painting her second bedroom. She had chosen a soft baby pink and lined the walls with a bright purple border. She found a white, gently used crib at the thrift store along with a very inexpensive daybed and mattress for Lacy.

After Emma and her mother moved past the initial shock, they too were on board loading down the spare room with countless toys, baby clothes, diapers, formula and even some special surprises for Lacy. When all was said and done the room was perfect. Claudia brought the final touch of an ultra fuzzy teddy bear to tuck in next to Lilly while she slept. In less than a week, Audrey, along with her family, had pulled it off, leaving the sweet new baby girl as the only missing piece.

Emma in particular was the most excited to welcome them home. She was rounded in a whole new way these days. Her baby bump was now holding an almost six month old little boy, apparently the size of a large mango and growing by the minute. She was no longer filled with morning sickness, only excitement as the weeks seemed to be flying by. Luke's room was finished also, covered in baby blue and chocolate brown paint with sock monkeys of every size lining the crib and adorning the walls. Alex had been kindly working fewer hours, taking her to her weekly doctor's appointments and helping prepare the house. He had already baby proofed every cabinet, toilet seat and door, although Emma had angrily reminded him they wouldn't need any of it for at least a year. She claimed to Audrey that he was completely out of control in the most adorable and

The Purpose

protective way. The new "Lacy and Lilly Effort" was aiding in keeping her mind focused only on extreme baby preparation in her own household.

Lacy was due to come home later in the evening and Audrey was a nervous wreck. She cleaned everything twice and had decorated the whole house in pink balloons and had ordered an oversized cake with real white and pink sugar icing. Someone had to help Lacy see that there was life after tragedy. She had considered inviting her mother, Emma and Claudia over for a grand welcome, but decided instead on it being just the three of them for their first night. There would several other opportunities to have a baby shower type gathering.

She borrowed Claudia's car to pick her up and before she left asked her to remind her one more time that she was doing the right thing. Smiling down on her, Claudia whispered, "There is no one I have met in all of my years with a kinder heart than you, sweet child." It was exactly what she needed to hear, but there was still something missing, or rather someone.

Lacy had been wheeled to the front entrance and was waiting patiently. Her nerves almost had the best of her, but every glance in Lilly's direction reminded her she was doing the right thing. Her ex had tried to call her cell phone seventy-three different times until she finally threw it into the toilet. She had felt so liberated at the sight of it floating in the water, never to be bothered by it again. It was by a miracle that she had chosen this hospital. It was over thirty miles from their tiny house and the last place he would

The Purpose

check. Besides, legally the hospital couldn't tell him if she had been admitted and there was comfort in that. Lilly was sleeping like an angel; she did most of the time. It was ninety-five degrees outside, but she still insisted on having her wrapped in a soft flannel blanket when she entered the world for the first time.

She looked exactly like Lacy, but her lips were identical to her father's and underneath them tucked the same chin dimple. She got only the best parts of him, she reminded herself. The bruising under her eyes had finally healed and she celebrated by putting on a fresh coat of mascara and smoothing on a peach lip stain. It was a new day and she was going to start over. He would never find them, and would more than likely eventually lose interest. At least she prayed he would.

Audrey came bounding through the door with a genuine and overjoyed grin from ear to ear at the sight of her two new best friends waiting in the lobby.

"I am so excited!" she yelled out before the sliding glass doors had the chance to open. Lacy laughed as she just saw her mouth open yelling out through the glass. When she finally stepped through, she repeated it over and over again. She squatted down and stroked Lilly's face and smiled up at Lacy. "This is going to be so great!"

Tucked safely in her new car seat, Lilly opened her eyes cautiously. Lacy and Audrey were chatting excitedly when Audrey noticed her from the rearview mirror. "Look, she is awake!"

Lacy spun around in her seat and smiled brightly. She

The Purpose

still wasn't quite used to seeing her. Sometimes it felt like she was dreaming, but there she sat wiggling her little fingers, smelling the fresh summer air. Lacy reached out and grabbed Audrey's hand. "In case I forget to tell you, thank you for saving us."

Lacy stood in awe of her new room. It was unreal how much Audrey had done for her. The most minor details were thought of, such as a toothbrush, socks, extra blankets and the most precious mobile for Lilly. Once she had settled her into the crib, she sat cross-legged on the floor and cried and cried. For once in over a year, she felt safe and protected. Everything really was going to be okay and if possible, she would find some way to repay Audrey. Someday, she would thank her.

Chapter 13

Several weeks later, Audrey walked Lacy down to the coffee shop and treated her to a warm breakfast and coffee. Lacy was gushing, her face filled with color and a healthy glow. Lilly cooed in the stroller as the sunlight beamed overhead.

"So what about you, Audrey? Any romantic interests?"

The question was so innocent, but loaded. If only she knew. "I guess you could say that I have had a few failed attempts."

"No no, not getting off that easily. Spill."

Audrey loved this side of her. She was feisty and spirited. "Well, you clearly know about Jason, but there is a certain someone."

"Ooo." Lacy stopped pushing the stroller for a moment to clap her hands.

"No 'oohing'," she said and laughed. "We grew up

The Purpose

together, kind of fell apart and recently became close again. I screwed it up pretty bad though; he moved away."

"Where did he go?"

"Well, we kissed only once, but I think he had too much wine and didn't really mean it. I fell for him so hard, so fast that it scared the hell out of me, you know? He is in his residency and headed to England to study at the beginning of the summer. He will probably be there for at least a year, so it really is hopeless."

Lacy looped her arm in Audrey's. "I am so sorry, girl; can't you call him?"

"I could." She sighed. "Trust me I have thought about it, but something stops me every time. Plus how would it ever work? I start school in the fall and he is just so far away."

"Love has a funny way of working through things. Whenever you give up, it seems to find you. You sound like you really love him."

"I do. I could never tell him though. I don't know if it's because of the whole Jason thing or what, but I am kind of nervous about trying again."

"What did you tell me the first day you met me?"

"I don't know." She scuffed her tennis shoes against the concrete.

"You told me to have faith in people. You have known him forever, evidently you trust him, but the question is whether or not you trust yourself."

That was the question. Maybe her issue with Will wasn't really his issue at all, rather her own? She had

The Purpose

forgiven herself and felt like she had really moved on, but had she really?

As the week wore on, Audrey watched in wonder as Lacy started to feel stronger and Lilly became more and more alert. Any chance she got, she would scoop her up and smother her in kisses. Claudia had even made it a regular routine to stop by and visit with her in the afternoons. There is something so special about a baby that brings out the best in everyone. Two weeks later, Lacy appeared in Audrey's door as she lay in bed reading, and said, "I am ready to work. Show me the way and I will get Lilly and me out of this mess."

The shelter was the perfect place for her. Lacy started out in reception at the beginning of the week and could be found cleaning out kennels and walking the dogs by Friday. She was impeccable for the job and took it more seriously than most of the regular employees. As visitors came in, she greeted them and Audrey saw the same spark that rested in her own eyes when she showed them around the shelter. It was like watching a kid go off to school for the first time, she had never felt so proud. Britney, from the shelter, even volunteered to babysit for her two times a week to help out and the rest of the time, Claudia watched over Lilly. The two of them together were quite the sight. They went for long walks, sat in the garden and Claudia read book after book to the tiny little infant. They were irresistibly adorable together and because Audrey trusted her, so did Lacy.

* * * *

The Purpose

One dreary afternoon, Audrey headed home slightly earlier than normal. Lacy was still finishing up, so she intended to surprise her with a great Italian dinner, spaghetti and meatballs. Comfort food was on the agenda, but then again, when was it not.

She was alarmed to hear Lilly crying with such intensity when she entered into the townhouse. Normally, Claudia would have calmed her before she could reach the point of shaking sobs. She picked up her pace on the stairs and flung open the front door to her apartment. Her eyes landed first on Lilly kicking her feet and throwing her fists into the air wildly from inside her crib, and then on the worst sight she had ever and would ever see again. It is like the world stops at a moment like this and the person involved has two choices; two incredibly quick, decisive choices. One can be brave and handle what needs to be accomplished, or fall apart and cry incessantly. Audrey, as attached to her new life as she was, decided to be brave for only a moment and then fall apart thereafter.

From where she stood at the front door, Lilly in her peripheral, she could see Claudia's 1920s red Mary Jane high heels lying flat on the floor from behind the kitchen counter. For that brief moment of strength, Audrey scooped up Lilly and slipped her finger in her mouth to soothe her, never removing her eyes from Claudia's shoes. Lilly ceased her hysteria, while Audrey's mounted as she rounded the corner and saw her lying flat on her back, eyes closed, holding a leaking baby bottle in one hand and a pink baby bib in the other. Audrey rushed toward her, attempting to

The Purpose

balance Lilly as she put her face to hers to listen for life, any sign at all.

Claudia, soft and peaceful, didn't stir. Her eyes remained sealed with her fluffy lashes fluttering above. Her landlord, her lifelike grandmother, her confidant, Bible study leader, fearless fairy Godmother and best friend were gone. If there is a word to describe what she felt at that moment, the only thing that comes to mind is anguish. It was as if someone ripped every bit of love and light in the world around her and sent it off to be with someone else.

Holding Claudia's hand and Lilly in the other arm, she closed her eyes letting silent tears roll down her cheeks, and felt life in all its forms pressing into her, new hope in one arm and the end of an era in the other. The only thing she felt was anguish, gut-wrenching, life-changing, misery seeking anguish.

The ambulance lifted her away, as Audrey, Lacy and Lilly clung to each other.

In the hours that followed, Lacy let Audrey be, seeing grief rippling across her face like waves to the shore. Claudia was intoxicating. Her love crept into your bones and lasted an eternity. Although Lacy had only known her for a matter of weeks, she was devastated.

Audrey sat in the corner of her room, no longer crying, but in shock. Her eyes closed, head tucked in her knees, she could only hear her missing laughter echoing throughout the bare walls. Words floated around her, such as "sweet darling" and "my child". It would be impossible to function

The Purpose

any time in the near future. When life steals a person like Claudia, a genuine mourning is necessary. In so many ways, she had saved her and without her guiding hand or support, she had little idea where to turn or what to believe in any more. Rocking back and forth, she begged for answers. Sending the questions out into the silence, praying someone could shed light.

"Claudia?" Her name came out as a sob. "If you can hear me, please know how I love you and forgive me for not telling you every day. I wish I would have known how little time I would have with you. I cherished every second of your lovable antics. You are so loved." She choked on her sob with the last word. "Please help me. I am so lost and confused on where I need to be and what I should do. You kept telling me that who I am would come to me and now I am left to figure it out on my own. Who am I kidding? I have two lives in my hands right now and I am incapable of taking care of myself." She fell forward on her knees and pressed her face against the cold, hardwood floor. "Please Claudia, help me. Don't leave just yet."

She hovered in this position until she fell into a shallow and lonesome sleep. Sorrow and devastation haunted her into her dreams and she clung to the floor. This house was the only remaining piece of Claudia. Even at her lowest point in her recently pitiful life, she never had felt as low as she did during that prayer.

Chapter 14

The following week was a blur. Lacy had agreed to help manage the shelter while Audrey was forced to meet with lawyers, as the remaining individual living in her estate. There were papers to sign, people to meet and then, of course, the funeral arrangements. Audrey intended to give her every bit of a proper farewell.

The bitter sounding lawyer grunted into her ear that he would be stopping by to see her later this afternoon and Audrey was panicking. It was only a matter of time before they had to vacate the premises, but Claudia had given her such an unreal rate for a two-bedroom that she surely couldn't afford anything more than a one-bedroom in town. She didn't have a car, so she couldn't be more than walking distance to the shelter. It was all so frustrating. She could barely keep her eyes from crying, let alone work out logistics. Lacy was her saving grace, keeping up with housework, cooking meals and working extra shifts at the shelter.

In the countdown of the final hours before the life-changing lawyer meeting, she scoured the internet looking for a new place. She wanted to sound confident, like she had everything under control. She poured over her budget, accounting for every last penny she had managed to save. At this point, she had a mere four hundred dollars in her savings, not quite enough to see them into a suitable place. Usually apartments had deposits, another thing Claudia had overlooked. Her efforts were hopeless. Everything on the market right now was more than twice what she could afford and even with Lacy pitching in, which she insisted on helping, it was virtually impossible.

Her doorbell sounded, followed by a stiff knock against the wooden door. It was now or never and she reminded herself of the greatest words Claudia had ever told her: "My dear," she whispered out loud, "life always has a way of working out."

She flung open the door to find a miniature version of a lawyer, easily standing a stout five feet tall at the most. His comb over started below one ear with only six or seven strands of hair bridging the gap, and his large, glassy eyes peered cautiously up at her through round, very thick glasses.

"Ms. Landrow?" he huffed, clearly out of breath.

"Yes, that is me. Won't you please come in?"

He scooted past her, in his version of a waddle, and plopped his briefcase down on her coffee table.

The Purpose

"Can I offer you something to drink? Coffee? Soda?"

"No."

She was annoyed immediately. This could make for a very sticky situation if she wasn't careful.

"Let's get to it."

"Okay, what is it that I can help you with? I realize that I probably have some sort of rights to exactly how many days I have to vacate. I mean, you have to understand that this is with such little warning and I need at least a few weeks to find a suitable place and afford the deposit on it. Not to worry, Mr. Pickleman, I have been looking."

He never raised his gaze, instead shifting his eyes back and forth through the paperwork. His lips mouthed the words, tiny pieces of spit shooting onto the paper.

"Not necessary," he finally muttered.

"I'm sorry?" she questioned, nervously biting her ring finger.

"She left you everything, Ms. Landrow, including her estate, her car and every bit of savings she had. It wasn't much, but it does rest in the less than ten thousand dollar range. She also outlined specific instructions on her hundreds of antiques, insisting that you hire her auctioneer who has already appraised everything at right under fifty-thousand dollars. She noted that you should do this instantly, but of course feel free to look through her belongings and keep what you would like."

Audrey's jaw had dropped, leaving her speechless. "She...she left it all to me?"

"Who else?" He finally met her gaze. "She had no one."

The Purpose

"That isn't true; she had so many people that loved her." His cold demeanor was beginning to get the best of her.

"Well no one that she loved more than you, I suppose." He softened, realizing the look of anger flashing across her restless eyes. She obviously hadn't slept in days.

"Thank you, Mr. Pickleman. I appreciate that." She lowered her head, as two single tears dripped onto her hands.

He continued, "She also specifically instructed me to educate you on the intent of her home. She precisely planned the use of it as the source of your new business. She didn't mention to me what type of business you had in mind, but only said that you had something in the works and her townhouse would be of great use to you in starting out."

Audrey looked puzzled, her mind fuzzy and struggling under the weight of exhaustion. "Business? I can't believe she remembered."

"Well, with all due respect, Ms. Landrow, she knew your intentions. Now no one will be here to monitor your use of the home, of course." He stared at her over his glasses. "Just make sure to honor her wishes."

"Yes, sir, of course."

He slammed the briefcase closed and stood.

"That's it? You're leaving?" she asked.

"What else do you need to know? We will continue with paperwork another time."

"I don't know. I am so confused with everything."

"I will give you a call and follow-up in a few days. For

now, make your way through her belongings and give this person a call." He slid a business card out from inside his tweed coat pocket. "He will get her antiques sold and give you some money to get things going. Oh one more thing." He stood up straighter than before and slipped his glasses off to wipe them clean on his white button-down shirt. "She doesn't want a traditional funeral and burial. She made it crystal clear that she intends to be cremated and have her ashes spread throughout the garden out back." He shuddered at the thought. "Don't know why that still gets to me. Anyways, she never was a traditional woman after all. Good day."

With that he scooted to the front door and made his way down the stairs one at a time. She could hear him whistling…disturbing. Such an odd, discomforting man had just delivered her from every bit of fear and anxiety she had. Nothing could replace her dear friend, but in so many ways she had planned all of this. She had intended all along to take care of her and see her dreams through. She had known her purpose all along and never felt the need to share them with her. She glanced upward. "Everything has a way of working out, just like you said, Claud."

In a fuzzy haze, she sat later that afternoon in the garden, with Lilly bouncing on her lap, telling Lacy of the unreal episode with the bizarre little lawyer.

"She left you everything? I can't believe it." Lacy sat scratching her head, just as awe-struck as Audrey. "What do you plan to do with all of it?"

Audrey wiped a bit of sleep from Lilly's eye and

continued rocking her back and forth. "I have an idea, but I don't know if I have the strength to pull it off. I am just so sad, you know?" She leaned her head back against the brick wall, trying to control her tears. The garden smelled so strongly of fresh summer soil and green leaves. Claudia had told her on several occasions that summer was her favorite season, that she loved the heat and passion of it, and so it only made sense that she chose that time to go.

"Are you going to be able to go through her things? I can't think of anything sadder." Lacy reached for Audrey's hand and squeezed it. "I'll help you, you know? Anything you need."

They sat in silence for a while, feeling Claudia surround them and wondering how particularly strange her death's timing actually was. She intended all of this, right down to the second. She knew that Audrey was ready to make some changes and get started on her dream, but didn't have the money to do so. She also knew how much Lilly and Lacy meant to her and how much they needed help, too. She literally had to have gone to the lawyer within the last few weeks. Do people really sense this sort of thing? Did she know she was about to leave them behind?

The wind picked up and ruffled Audrey's curls and the few strands of soft hair on Lilly's head. The sound of the weeping willow was comforting. The magic of the woman Claudia really was and what others thought of her was beyond an understatement. She was in so many ways an inspiration.

* * * *

The Purpose

Several days later, Audrey was still resisting the notion of going through Claudia's things. She could barely even look at her door as she passed by it on the way to work. It was a certain phone call that prompted her to even consider it.

"Hey, kid." Will's voice was raspy, exhausted.

Audrey's heart almost beat out of her chest. He still cared about her.

"Will, it is so good to hear your voice."

"My dad called me about Claudia. Listen, I am really sorry you have to go through this. You have been through enough."

"Thanks, it is really the saddest thing I have ever gone through. I still cry all the time." She squeezed the phone, urging him with her thoughts to keep talking. It didn't matter what he had to say, she just needed him.

"I wish I could offer to help, but I am a little too far away."

"Yeah." She listened for him to go on.

"What is this about you taking in an abused woman and her baby? Am I really getting that right?"

"It seems crazy, I know, but have you ever felt like you didn't have any choice but to do the right thing? I mean, when you meet her someday, you will see. She is amazing and I couldn't leave her in a shelter somewhere."

"First dogs, now people. Guess I shouldn't have expected anything else." He chuckled.

She laughed too.

"I am pretty lucky to have her here. She is so good to

The Purpose

me, a best friend really. Plus, I don't know where I would be without her right now."

"I am glad you have someone. Well, listen…"

No, he was going to hang up. She had been waiting for this call for what felt like years. She needed to prolong the conversation. She needed to know if he had found anyone else to help him forget about her.

"Um, Will?"

"Yeah?"

A long pause; she could hear his breathing.

"We miss you around here."

Another moment of silence.

"Miss you guys, too. Really, I do. Call you later, k?" She heard laughter in the background.

She hung up, knowing he wouldn't. There was still so much awkwardness between them. Even if she had wanted to say what she was feeling, how could she send her heart's aching desperation for him to love her down the line of a phone call. She imagined the adorable little English nurse sitting right next to him, urging him to hang up the phone so they could go grab a bite to eat. At the thought of her saying "bite to eat" she melted under the sadness of Claudia's equally adorable imposter English accent.

Things had to get better. Life had to get better. She couldn't possibly face another year of this impounding sense of doom and loneliness. If it killed her, she would find a way to lift her from below the mound of disappointment. It was time her damn lemonade was squeezed out of the thousands of lemons handed to her. The only thing that

The Purpose

mattered was her life now. No one else can possibly make someone happy. It is a personal mission, an entirely selfish passage. *Bring it on.*

Emma agreed to help her sort through Claudia's past. She needed her sister, now more than ever. Hand in hand, they eased open the door to her townhouse and held their breath before entering. Audrey's heart was pounding. She had been in her home a hundred times before, but this time she wouldn't be there. She wouldn't come breezing through the doorway insisting on making hot tea with a splash of lemon and a pinch of sugar. She wouldn't run her fingers through Audrey's long hair, insisting on hearing every detail of her day. She wouldn't be smothered in various shades of paint, and the worst part of all was the way the apartment smelled. It used to be filled with the scent of mixed oil paints and fresh gingersnap cookies topped with powdered sugar for a "kick", but now it only held a tang of abandonment, stale even.

The whole apartment was still neat and tidy; that was one thing Claudia was known for. She knew how to keep an immaculate house. Image wise, she was consistently a wild disorderly mess, but her home always sparkled. On many occasions, she could be found scrubbing the hardwood floor or polishing the silver fixtures in the bathroom. Not even a month after she had passed, it was still spotless.

Emma walked slowly behind Audrey, allowing her to have her moment with what was left with Claudia's memory. She watched with tears teetering on the edge of overload as Audrey skimmed her hand along countertops,

The Purpose

gently over paintings and thoughtfully over snapshots captured in crystallized frames. A shell of a home that once was filled with boundless spouts of laughter, now sat empty and alone. It was as if the house itself was lost without her. Emma took in the look of heartbreak and abandonment twisting Audrey's normally flawless face into torment.

Life happens and everyone loses people they love, but the question was left unanswered by every member of their family; why Audrey? Hadn't she been through enough? It was as if life was hell-bent on bringing her down. Yet, Emma witnessed her spirit at its strongest, seeing her roam from room to room, calm and still. It was impossible to break her, like an uncultivated and untamed warrior horse galloping through the wind and rain among the sloping hills of the West. Try as life may to strap a saddle to her back and force her into a fenced pen, taking away the beauty and freedom of the journey, she would always fight for redemption. She would always win.

Emma sat poised on the couch in the center of the room, awaiting further instructions, when she heard Audrey's gasp from across the hall.

"Everything okay in there?" she called out.

"Emma, look at this. I can't believe it."

Audrey emerged carrying one of Claudia's countless paintings. She turned it around for Emma to see. Awestruck, she reached out to touch it. The fluid strokes of only the brightest colors: pink, purple, silver and white outlined a portrait of her sweet sister. She wasn't looking straight ahead, but rather her head was tilted down, her face filled with laughter. It was a sensitive portrait, showcasing Audrey's raw emotion. Her personality had always been peaceful, serene, and this painting captured it. Her smile was broad and her dimple on display. Small tendrils of blonde hair fell around her face, leaving her frozen in time, content in the moment.

"Audrey," she lifted her hand to swipe tears from her cheeks, "it is stunning."

"It looks just like me." She couldn't take her eyes off of it. The lines of her eyes, the tip of her nose, it was her through and through. "I didn't even know she was painting it. Why do you think she never gave it to me?"

Emma knew why. It was obvious. Claudia had been a seamstress of life's emotions and always chose to weave her opinions in at the appropriate times. Audrey's face forced her to resist answering the question. It was something she needed to figure out on her own. "I'm not sure. Maybe she was going to give it to you soon."

"Maybe." She pulled the painting to her, holding it tightly. "I can imagine her painting it, the look on her face. She was so vulnerable when she was in the moment, covered in paint and completely engrossed in her work. Beautiful."

She looked over it again, her eyes lingering. "I always wondered how she would paint me. She said to me once that she did her best to capture people's true personality, whether it was ambitious, cynical, observant or insane. She wasn't afraid to paint the reality. I loved her for that. I just wish I knew what she was trying to capture with me."

The Purpose

Emma stood quietly, wishing she could see what she saw. Jason had lifted any confidence from her demeanor years ago. It pained her to see her sister without a dash of self-esteem any more. Growing up, she had always been the center of attention without ever trying to be. She could own a room by simply walking in it and regardless of what was going on around her, when she talked to you, it was as if you were the only one in the room. She was remarkable, not just beautiful, but breathtaking, and she could never see it when she glanced in the mirror. There are beautiful people, symmetrically perfect in every way, and then there are women who belong on the red carpet being fawned over and idolized.

In the last nine months, she had blossomed into what she was always intended to be and yet, she still felt so inadequate and insufficient. No matter how many times her mother, father or any man she had ever dated complimented her, she only saw what Jason insisted upon in the mirror.

"I think she was trying to capture the way you make people feel. You have always and will always be impossible not to love."

Her sister was being kind, another typical trait. She always had a way of saying the perfect thing when someone needed a boost. She prided herself on consistently offering unyielding support. Her belly bump poked out from her yellow tank top with her tanned arms resting on top.

"Thanks, Em, I needed that." It was so nice to have unity for once. So often they could rattle each other and create friction when it was least needed. At this moment,

The Purpose

surrounded by the memory of a woman who showed them how to live with integrity and humility, they were sensitive to one another and modest in the most comforting way.

They focused their pent-up, stressful energy for the next five hours on sorting, organizing, categorizing, stacking, recording and boxing all of Claudia's things. They hand-selected the things of value or sentiment they personally wanted to keep and carefully packed up the rest. They took down her paintings, folded her blankets, packed her pots and pans and tucked away her old photographs. Audrey was so focused on doing things the proper way that she literally zoned out, forgetting what her mission was in the first place. It almost felt surreal, as if she were packing up a stranger's home, someone she barely knew.

At times she would pause her distraction mode and try on one of Claudia's feather hats or slip into a pair of her heels, but then with a rush of the same heart-wrenching anguish, she would flashback to the site of her red Mary Jane shoes lying on the cold wooden floor the day she passed. With every jar of her memory, a pain would erupt and hover somewhere between her chest and her head. This truly was the hardest thing she ever had to do.

Emma had lain down to rest her eyes. She was easily exhausted these days and rightfully so. Audrey tiptoed around her and pulled out the photo album resting on a stack of books in an open box. She peeled back the cover. The plastic stuck a bit, aged with time. The first picture was of Claudia and her mother. She had never seen this picture; somehow with the hours spent combing through her

The Purpose

memory books, this particular album never surfaced. She couldn't help but wonder if it was too dear to her heart to share. She flipped another page and found Claudia, tall, gangly and holding a stack of school books. Her smile was from ear to ear, just like always.

The pictures continued on until she flipped to the final page of the album. A neatly folded letter was pressed under the plastic with ink pen scribbled across. The person who wrote it obviously carefully selected their words and spent a great deal of time on their penmanship. The letter read:

Dear Claudia,

You have never been as lovely as you were last night. My breath escaped me when you entered the room and my heart felt as if it might leap right out of my chest. How did I ever get so lucky as to love you?

You said something to me that resonated with my soul. Do you remember what it was dear? You told me you planned on loving me forever. For some reason, I will never forget what you said. Although you had one too many glasses of wine, sweet darling, you meant it. I could see it in your eyes. I could feel it in your kiss.

So here is my vow, let me grow old with you. Let me kiss you under every sunset and let me hold you as every star emerges in the dark night.

The Purpose

Plan to love me forever and I will never let you go.

Kisses~
Frank

Audrey covered her mouth in awe. She said they only had a love affair of three months. He was over the moon and then some for her. He loved her! They had the kind of passion every couple dreams of. She made it appear she had dismissed him when he became too much, heading to England under false promises. If only she could have told her the real ending to the story. This letter revealed so much more than she ever did.

She shook Emma gently, dying to share the story with her. Emma rose from the couch, scratching at her head, struggling with being woken up.

"Can I help you?"

Audrey shook the letter at her. "Read it!"

Emma scooted forward on the couch toward her, belly first. "Well, don't make me work for it or anything." She wrinkled her nose and squinted her eyes at her.

Letter in hand, she leaned back against the couch and read each word carefully, eyes growing larger by the second.

"Oh my Lord, this is…this is Frank Sinatra!"

"Well, yeah! Don't you see though? She always made it seem so innocent, like they had such a short, unconnected time together."

The Purpose

"Yeah?" Emma questioned, a smirk spreading across her face.

"This letter doesn't agree. They clearly had an extremely passionate affair, deeply in love!"

"Or, and it could go either way really, maybe Frank was more in love with her than she was with him."

"How do you figure?" Audrey's eyebrows lowered, her voice deepening.

"He said 'you had one too many glasses of wine'…maybe she just said those things because she was drunk."

Audrey rose to her feet, her pulse quickening.

"Or maybe, the truth finally came out when she had enough liquid courage."

"You think so?" Emma cocked her head sideways. "You think she really meant it?"

"Yes I do." She stomped her foot, grabbing the letter back. She scanned it, searching for more clues. "She loved him and he loved her. No one feels this way about someone else only one-sided. You can tell when someone loves you like this." She sat down into the arm chair, eyes never lifting from the letter.

"Well then, what the hell are you waiting for?"

Audrey lifted her gaze to Emma who was beaming, eyes filled with sparkle. "What?"

"Will meant that kiss, Audrey. You know it, so go tell him that you feel the same way and for the love of God, help me get up from this couch."

Emma's words clung to her like a bad cold. She was

The Purpose

right, as always. But today wasn't about that. Today was only for Claudia. Everyone in her family had offered to join her in spreading the ashes throughout the garden, but she reverently declined. She needed to stand on her own two feet right now and do this for her friend. She stood barefoot, like Claudia always did in the garden. She wiggled her toes and felt the dry dirt smooth the bottoms of her feet. There was a gentle wind and the sun had respectfully tucked itself behind a cloud, allowing for a moment of gloom.

She crouched down to her knees, clutching the urn. It was cold against her body, reminding her of every bit of the contents inside. She closed her eyes and prayed. She prayed to God, prayed to Claudia. There was so much to say, but she delivered a meaningful promise to fulfill every bit of her destiny in her honor.

She opened the lid, leaned forward to allow the ashes to spill into the garden bed, and softly, she began to sing aloud, "Just a turn to the right, you find a little white light. It will lead to my little blue heaven. You see a smiling face, a fireplace, a cozy room. A little nest nestled where the roses bloom. Just Lacy and me, and a baby makes three. We're happy in my little blue heaven."

The pieces drifted through the air like tiny grains of sand as she sang; floating up, up and away into the sky to watch over her. Claudia now rested where she was always meant to be, partially on earth and ultimately in Heaven.

"Goodbye, my sweet darling."

Chapter 15

Later that afternoon, Lacy headed in for another follow-up appointment, while Audrey looked over Lilly. She walked her down to the river, letting the flowing water help her mind drift away with it. She cuddled with her on the couch and sang to her while her eyes fought sleep the way only an infant can do. She was so beautiful and being with her made everything else seem not quite so bad. Her little finger clung on to hers, small and wrinkled. She was what life was all about.

When she laid her down in her crib for her mid-afternoon nap, she stood impatiently in the living room, looking around. "Will meant that kiss…"

Emma's words led her to her closet and forced her to grab her suitcase.

"Now go get him…" She lifted her passport from the drawer beside her bed. She only had one stamp in it, a family

The Purpose

trip to Mexico six years back. The sun had been strong on a white beach with teal water splashing playfully at her feet while she and Emma lay out for hours. Covered in part sun block and part tanning oil, they ended up looking like raccoons and unable to take a shower for three days because of their overly toasted skin. They walked the beach at night, drank virgin daiquiris by day, and their father had even paid for horseback riding on the beach. She could still hear her mother's screams as she lifted from the vast glass ocean surface in her roaring jet ski. She would give anything to go back to Mexico. It was a simpler time, before Jason had stormed into her life, erasing all beauty and peace.

Mexico sounded pleasant, but England was holding her heart for ransom. One by one she layered dresses, jeans, t-shirts, night clothes, socks, shoes, hair and makeup essentials into a black suitcase with purple hearts. She zipped it closed, sat it by the front door and picked up the phone to call her mother.

"Hi, sweetheart, how are you?"

"I am getting stronger each day, tired of feeling so down." Audrey's voice was soft and timid.

"Is there anything you need, honey? I can come over if you want some company."

"Actually, I thought I should call before I leave the country."

"What? Where are you going? Don't do anything crazy, Audrey Mae."

"No, Mom, I am finally seeing clearly. Life is too short, you know? I learned that this year. Everyone around me is battling serious issues, and I have stood by on the sidelines allowing life to circle around me, instead of jumping into the crazy mess that it always will be."

"Where are you going with this?" Her voice verged on hysteria.

"England. I am going to England to tell the man I have loved since I can remember. It has always been him and it took tragedy and the fear of losing him to realize it."

"We knew it! Mark said something at the party and your father and I haven't stopped talking about it! Oh. Audrey, he is the one. I think I have known that all along."

"You think so?" She perked up a little. Maybe it wasn't all in her head.

"Damn straight, girl. I'll even go with you if you want."

She laughed. Her mother had never cursed in all her years. It was oddly refreshing.

"Thanks, I appreciate it. Really I do. I'll be fine, don't worry."

"You are always fine. Remember that, if anyone has a fighting chance at getting what she wants, it is you." She smiled through the phone line. "Call me anytime."

"K, Mom. Love you."

"Love you more."

"Hey, Mom?"

"Yeah?"

"What if he doesn't feel the same way?" Finally, she said the question out loud, confirming her gut-wrenching fear.

"Impossible."

The Purpose

* * * *

Lacy came home exhausted and feeling slightly nauseas, but her face lit up at the sight of Audrey's suitcase by the door. She even managed to jump up and down slightly. "Finally! I thought this day would never come!" Without looking back, she closed the door behind her, climbed in Claudia's car and headed for the airport, remembering, no one else can possibly make someone happy. It is a personal mission, an entirely selfish passage.

She had to wait two and a half hours for a flight to Chicago, IL. From Illinois onto London, England, of which would be an eight and half hour flight and then a train ride from London to Norwich thereafter. It was a good thing that she brought her laptop, seeing as it was the absolute perfect time to start writing. She settled into the corner of the café in the airport and pulled Frank's letter out of her pocket. It was her permanent reminder that not only did true love really exist, but she was tossed into it, never to look back. She was in love, mind-boggling, heart-drawing on your notebook love and everyone around her knew before she did. Did that mean that Will already knew? Was he waiting for her to figure it out?

A woman in her mid-forties sat down across from her at a different table and slung her carry-on bag on it with a loud thump. Her hair was chopped neatly in a bob with equally precise bangs strung across her forehead. She sighed, looked around and eventually rested her eyes on Audrey. She

The Purpose

smiled, revealing a small amount of lines around the corners of her eyes and mouth.

"How long do you have to wait?" she asked politely.

"Another two hours. How about you?" Audrey tucked the letter back in her pocket and straightened up in her chair.

"Same. I am heading to Ireland to visit family, flight was delayed."

"Wow, that sounds really exciting! I have never been."

"It would be exciting if I didn't have to deal with such a delay. Guess family is worth it though, right?"

"Absolutely." She grinned. "Nothing more important."

"Where are you headed?"

"England. Visiting a friend."

"Does he live there?" She raised her thin, straight eyebrows.

"He is studying at the University Hospital over there." She hesitated to sound foolish, but the woman persisted.

"He? Is it someone you're dating?" Her smile grew larger.

"I wouldn't say that. Maybe someone I am trying to date." She blushed.

The woman stood up, grabbed her bag and plopped down in front of Audrey. "I am Georgia….tell me everything! I am in need of a juicy story!"

Life was well beyond the awkward phase. Nothing surprised Audrey any longer and she opened up like a tulip in the springtime about growing up together, how he had been there for her and how she let him go. She left nothing to the

The Purpose

imagination, watching Georgia's eyes grow with each detail.

"Incredible! How can you possibly think he doesn't love you back? You're obviously meant to be; I mean are you listening to yourself?" She leaned back in her chair, snagged a sip of her latte, clearly pleased with herself. "This is like out of a movie or something, you going after him. I wish I could be there!"

Audrey laughed in spite of herself; this clingy woman was the exact dose of distraction and confidence she was in need of. Georgia had found herself in the right place at precisely the perfect time.

Chapter 16

Eleven and a half hours later, Audrey stumbled off the plane. She was utterly exhausted, even though she had slept through the last half of the plane ride. She was currently six hours ahead of time from St. Louis and she felt every second of it.

She realized as she rolled her suitcase through the airport that she had little to no plan. As far as she could see, she would board the train to Norwich, find the hospital and spout off about love and being meant to be once she found him. What if he wasn't working? Where would she stay? What if it were the wrong hospital? She had tried to dial her mother and Emma again to verify, but the connection was impossible back to the states. Plan or not, it was too late now.

Directions from a tall, lanky woman behind the service desk led her to a taxi cab and then on to a train station. London passed her by through the windows in all its grandeur. It was breathtaking, and all the while she remembered Claudia with each piece of the city. This was her mother ship, her home. She had intentionally asked the cab driver to take the longest route possible, one that would indeed lead her past the London Eye and Big Ben. They called to her, begged for her to leap out of the cab and snap hundreds of pictures, but not today. There would be another time for that. Right now, she needed to get to Will.

The train ride was brief, delivering her right on time to her destiny. As the doors pulled open with a loud whishing sound, she shuddered, unable to comprehend making it this far. One foot in front of the other was the only way she could ever make it to the hospital, to her Will. She slung her oversized bag into yet another cab and pulled out her makeup case. She looked atrocious, comparable to that night in the hospital when he came back into her life. He had looked through her with those endearing eyes, begging to be let in and she pushed him away once again. She always did that; no wonder he left.

Lip-gloss, a fresh coat of deodorant, despite the grimace from the British cab driver, and a little blush, and she was ready to face him. She had convinced herself and written in her journal that no matter what he said, no matter how this all ended up, she was doing the right thing. He needed to hear this from her before she started a life without him. After all, that is what true love is really all about. Right? Life's purpose, even if she struggled with her own, was to love someone with all of your heart, expecting nothing in return. She needed to spread her love across the

The Purpose

ocean, throughout the cities that separated them and into his world. Whether he wanted it or needed it, she had to share it. *Ready or not, here comes love…*

* * * *

The cab came to a rolling halt and the driver whirled around in his seat, arm extended. She laid the cash into it and reached for her bag. She couldn't open the door. She was paralyzed; much like the night he left her frozen in her bedroom, unable to stop him. The cab driver continued to eye her from the front seat as she stared blankly at the hospital.

"You said Norfolk & Norwich University Hospital, right?" he mumbled.

"Yes, yes I did."

"Well then?" He lifted a hand impatiently.

She continued to stare, eyes wider than a child on Christmas morning.

He waited another moment before sighing loudly, flinging open his door, walking around and then ripping her door open, fresh air collapsing into her.

"Miss?" He lowered his head down, gently removing his cap. Suddenly he was a gentleman.

She stretched her legs out of the side of the cab and slowly slid toward the exit, all the while staring nervously ahead at the looming hospital. It was immense, part modern with glass buildings and part old England, with cathedral towers. She was calmed by the presence of greatness in medicine as she continued to slide, very slowly.

The Purpose

Feet firmly planted on the concrete entrance to the hospital, she stood, blood rushing to her head. She had a brief flashback of the time she passed out and steadied herself to make sure it didn't happen again. She nodded at the cab driver and started toward the entrance.

"No matter what," she spoke out in a whisper, "you are doing the right thing."

"Can I help you?" An English voice flustered her train of thought. She focused in on a small framed, beautiful woman with freckles. *Amazing*, she thought. *How on earth did this woman look exactly like the nurse she pictured Will falling in love with?*

"I..." she stuttered. "I am trying to find Will Michaels. He is here from America, a part of a work study program."

"Oh Will, curly hair?" Of course she knew him. Probably knew the way he kissed, too.

"Yes." She smiled, attempting to be polite. "That is him."

"I can have him paged if you'd like. He should still be around here somewhere."

"Yes, thank you." Audrey straightened her sundress out, noticing suddenly the countless amount of wrinkles embedded from the journey. She heard the English woman's voice call out over the pager system, "Paging Dr. Will Michaels to the lobby, Dr. Michaels." He was considered a doctor now, a thought she had yet to truly embrace. Little Will from the tree house with a fire-red cape flying behind him was a doctor?

She heard him paged again, and finally a third time,

The Purpose

before the phone at the front desk rang loudly. Audrey could hear her whispering quietly into the phone before she slammed it on the receiver and stood up to see her sitting in the lobby.

"Sorry, he has already left for the evening," she called out.

"Oh, is there anyone that can tell me where he is staying, by chance? I have come all the way from America to see him."

"Sorry. We are unable to release any sort of personal information about our staff. You can always try again tomorrow. He comes in at ten."

"Thank you. I will do that."

Feeling defeated, terrified and ironically giddy, she made her way back outside with her suitcase rolling behind her. He was in this town, less than a mile away probably. All she had to do was pick up her cell phone and dial the number she had dialed a million times. Yet, this journey wasn't about a phone call. She could have placed that call about twelve hours ago and gotten everything off of her chest. This conversation needed to be done in person, where she could reach out and run her fingers along his strong jaw and gaze lovingly into his eyes. He was minutes away, possibly in the hotel just around the corner, but she could force herself to wait one more night. After all, she was in the most adorable town in the world, her eyes had just noticed. Spending a night in a fairy tale of a city couldn't make it any worse or harder. If anything, a good night's sleep, a hot bath and a warm meal could make what she had

The Purpose

to say feel more premeditated.

Norwich, England, was colorful and rich with energy. It was charming and held mystery of medieval times. Tiny cafes, book stores and bistros were tucked in around the cobblestone streets. She could literally feel years of love lost and love found nestled in corners of rustic signs and enchanting bridges. She chose a hotel by the name of "Maids Head Hotel", obviously noting an intriguing story must be lurking behind the name. It was built in the 13th century and now rested as an historic part of Norwich.

No wonder Will had chosen this part of the world to slip into for the next year. There was even a castle, by the name of Norwich Castle proudly on display directly across from her hotel. She promised herself as she sat gazing out of her precious hotel's window that even if things went wrong with Will tomorrow, that she would take time to indulge in at least one cup of English tea and then traipse around in that magnificent castle tomorrow. It isn't every day a girl gets to soak up a castle.

Jonathan, the gray haired Disney-looking character working the front desk of the hotel, insisted she stay in the Queen Elizabeth suite. She had mentioned she was only there for one evening and because it was a generally slow weekend, she could take the suite at a discount. Her jaw fell to the floor as she entered the room, doing a double take at the beautifully exposed oak wooden beams throughout the lounge and bedroom. Jonathan carried her bags into the room, all the while explaining the furniture was from the 16th century and that she was a part of its history now.

The Purpose

"Please, Madame, I do hope you'll take a sample of our delectable dinner course this evening. We offer over forty wines at any given time. I assure you, you will most certainly find something to your liking." He bowed at the waist, sweeping his oversized hands in a circle as he stepped out of her suite. She turned round and round when the door closed, dancing on her tippy toes. Everyone in their life needs to stay in the Queen Elizabeth suite; it was breathtaking.

She carefully laid out her clothes, and then hung them one by one on the hangers in the armoire. It was nine o'clock in England and although her eyes were drooping, those forty flavors of wine were calling her name. She splashed some water on her face and ran a brush through her hair before heading downstairs. She was more than capable of dining alone; women in the movies did it all the time and usually found interesting people to talk to. If only Will had been working, then this could be a reunion dinner, a celebration. Instead, it was the interlude to her impulsive journey.

"Welcome to *Wine Press*, Madame. I am Perry and I will be taking care of you this evening. Are we expecting another guest?" The waiter was easily two or three years older than Audrey; oddly he seemed far beyond his age. He peered at her anxiously, expecting her to insist he leave the silver and wineglass behind, her date would be arriving shortly. She smiled and said, "No, I am on my own this evening. Prepare to spoil me with your best champagne."

Unexpectedly, he laughed out loud, wiping tears from the corners of his eyes. "Indeed, Miss…"

"Audrey," she said and grinned. "My name is Audrey."

The Purpose

"Miss Audrey, prepare to be spoiled."

He returned moments later with a glass of bubbly and strawberries spread on dry toast.

"Miss Audrey, please enjoy our finest *Champagne Tattinger;* it is a brut reserve from the rolling hills of France. It is complemented this evening by sweet, scintillating strawberries spread on a splendid toast."

She nodded, reaching for the champagne. If she blinked and opened her eyes to Richard Gere, it wouldn't be a surprise. So much of *Pretty Woman* had become her life during this trip.

The remainder of her meal was equally as thrilling. Next came a salad of jersey royals, purple sprouting broccoli with smoked garlic dressing and cool cucumber soup. It was followed by fresh angel hair pasta, mixed with peas, charred artichokes and cherry tomatoes. She was on champagne glass number three by the time she reached the most delectable dessert ever known to man, dark chocolate risotto with amoretti and orange shortbread. She smiled as she scooped minute bites into her watering mouth, ensuring she tasted every rip-roaring morsel.

Audrey sipped the final bubble from her fluted glass and looked around the room. She had been so hungry, that she had not yet noticed the glamorous beauty she had become a temporary fixture in. The ceiling was purely a collection of window panes, allowing the stars to set the tone and generate English ambiance. The walls were stone and encrusted with historic statues of women in lovely gowns and men with swords. There was a boulder water

The Purpose

fountain in the middle of the room that held only candles instead of water and they illuminated the entire room. The crowd had thinned considerably while she devoured the best meal she had ever experienced, and now she sat slightly tipsy in a corner, waiting for her kind and generous waiter, Perry, to return.

He never did and so she made her way to the front desk and gave the tiny silver bell a ring. Jonathan rounded the corner and instantly smiled at the sight of the flushed blonde girl he had escorted hours prior.

"Miss?" He chuckled.

"Oh hi, Jonathan. I have lost my waiter and I am the only one left in the restaurant." She hiccupped loudly and it echoed throughout the empty foyer.

"Ah yes, Miss Landrow. Perry insisted this evening was his treat. Consider us squared away."

Hiccup. "Why would anyone do that?"

"Everyone needs a friend." He smiled and slipped behind the doorway to keep from embarrassing her further.

She walked in a rather amusing pattern, side to side, holding the walls for support as she made her way back to Queen Elizabeth's suite. She laughed quietly to herself, or at least she thought it was quietly, at the karma of it all. It was those very words that she had said to Lacy months ago.

A bed filled with six overly-stuffed pillows, thrilling silk sheets and a lush down comforter folded her into its arms and whisked her away to charming Norwich dreams, one hiccup at a time.

Chapter 17

Despite the bubbles floating in her head, she woke with pure satisfaction. Today was the day she would announce to the world, more importantly Will, that she was in love. It didn't matter what she wore, how much makeup she had on or even what she said. Ultimately, he had seen her at every level of her lowest point and if he loved her, the only thing that mattered was her being there.

She sat waiting for what felt like the hundredth time in a hospital while he was paged. It was a splendid day in England and people could be seen walking by on the streets, playful children running alongside them. The trees were lustrous shades of green and she imagined how it must be to paint them on a canvas. She would use lime, forest and the palest green available.

She tapped her ballet flats against the floor to the beat of the song overhead, picturing the way Will danced with her the last time they saw each other. Frank wrote of feeling

The Purpose

your heart leap and her heart not only leapt, but sprung right out of her chest and across the spacious sea.

"Audrey?"

She looked up, stepped out of her memories and into the real world. He was headed toward her, not at all like she imagined. She had a mental image of Will being glamorous and seductive when they finally met. He would pull her into his arms and kiss her along her cheeks, forehead and finally lips. This Will did not look like he was ready to be kissed or do the kissing. He was clearly exhausted, wiped clean of any energy he had packed in his suitcase alongside his surgical scrubs. His usual scruff had almost reached a full grown beard and his eyes had lost their luster, hovering above vague puffy bags. Forget any idea of him not being beautiful as always, but it was painful to see him at a breaking point.

She reached for him and he hugged her tightly.

"What are you doing here? My God, it is so good to see you. Is everything okay?"

She pulled on his hand toward the door. "Can we go somewhere and talk for a moment?"

"Yeah, really, is everything all right?"

"Fine, Will." She ruffled his curls which had outgrown even his tolerable length. "Let's just go sit outside in the city of Norwich and talk for a bit." She flashed him the most uplifting smile she had tucked in her back pocket. She was giddy and she couldn't hide it.

They settled in to a park bench across the street with a parade of multi-colored vibrant flowers swarming around them. If she inhaled just right, she could smell all of them at

The Purpose

once. Will never removed his eyes from her, squeezed her hand and asked again, "What's going on?"

She took a deep breath as if trying to take in all of the confidence from passersby.

"You look exhausted by the way," she said and laughed nervously.

He lowered his eyebrows and grunted, "Any day now."

"Will, this is the hardest thing I have ever had to say, so please just listen open-ended without judgment or input until I have completely winded every thought floating through my wild imagination."

His eyes widened. "Dear Lord, Audrey. What is it?"

"Do you remember how Claudia told me to find my purpose?"

"Yeah?" His eyes softened.

"I have spent almost an entire year frantically searching for clues. I struggled to believe in myself again and begged for answers to questions I didn't even understand. I befriended characters in my story that opened doors for me and helped me close others. I even fell in love." She looked down to her fingers and circled her thumb around her sapphire ring.

"The point is that I have been searching for so long to find...well, me. I needed to know who I was before I could ever dream of finding happiness again. I have found it, Will. I have fallen into the hands of my greatest purpose and I needed to tell you that. I needed you to know that the hours of tears, confusion and frustration have finally revealed exactly where I belong."

The Purpose

Her eyes misted over and she reached for his hands. His mouth opened slightly. He listened with every corner of his heart.

"The best part of it is, I went searching for one answer and I found two. Will, you are the first answer, the final answer and every silly answer in between. I am in love with you." She pulled in a long drawn out breath and let it go, like releasing a mended eagle into the wild. Even if the release is expected, it is still remarkable and stunning. She looked up to see tears on the brim of Will's exhausted and worn face. He didn't reply, didn't breathe, and didn't blink; instead, he reached for her, sliding across the bench until their faces were inches apart.

"You said you found two answers?" He lifted his hands to meet her cheeks and wiped tears away gently.

"Oh that." She laughed, flustered. "I am going to open a women's shelter. I have a million ideas on how to keep hurt and abused women safe."

He pulled her face to his, lips only half an inch apart. "If anyone can do it, it is you, kid."

With that, he sealed the miles and hours between them with time's most perfect kiss. They leaned into one another and all of the days leading up to this moment swirled around them. The moments lying by the pond counting stars, the hours chasing each other through open fields, the days writing letters while they were grounded, the years loving one another in utter belief that one day, this day, it would be met with an endearing, long-awaited, soul-searching kiss. He didn't have to say anything. He just needed to fill the

The Purpose

void of fear, disbelief and doubt with the warmth only a kiss can bring.

They held each other for a long time, her crying softly into his strong body and him pulling her tighter with each tear of joy that fell upon his shoulder.

As they walked hand in hand back toward the hospital, he stopped in his tracks, eyes on the sky. He looped his arm around her shoulder and turned her to face him.

"Something's on my mind, kid, has been for a long time."

"Oh?" She smiled sweetly.

"Yeah, you have been on this mission from the Heavens to find your purpose, but all the while you have been missing something."

"What?" Her eyes focused in, serious taking over as the primary expression.

"It's just that, well, you claim you couldn't figure out where you basically belong, but the thing of it is," he held her face in his hands, "your purpose has always been being the only light in the world so many can see for miles. You bring joy, Audrey, light and love to those around you. Your heart is so damn big that it can hold everyone and anyone it meets. You take in stray animals, stray people and fall in love with the most intriguing individuals that others would disregard. You have always seen the best in people and that is why *I* love you."

There it is, she thought, *the reason he was made for me.*

* * * *

The Purpose

They spent the next few days snuggling in his equally oversized, fluffy bed, kissing each other hundreds of times, as if wondering whether or not it would be their last. He had permission to take a few days from the hospital to visit with his out of town guest and he was bound and determined to make the best of it. His Audrey had found him and finally figured out what their little misstep of a dance had always led to. He waited patiently while she ran circles around her final destination. He watched as she fumbled and questioned, never faulting to the idea of a life without her.

When he watched her pretend to sleep, lying in bed the night he left, his heart twisted at the idea of leaving her, but he knew it had to be done. There wasn't anything he could do to help her love herself again. That smug, arrogant bastard had destroyed the beauty in her version of the world and she needed to find it again on her own. It mattered little to him how long it would take. He had loved her patiently since high school, pretending she was only a childhood friend. The clues he gave her along the way were never recognized and if he had pushed, she would have resisted. Audrey had always done things in her own time and on her own accord. Loving him was no different.

Now she slept, curled in a burrito of a blanket, eyes fluttering as she dreamed. She was beyond beautiful, she was striking, a word he designated only for her. He knew it was a disservice to him not to log as many hours of sleep as possible while she too slept, but he couldn't take his eyes off of her. He had spent days wandering the streets of Norwich, lost without her. He had envisioned this trip for so

The Purpose

many years. He had practically tasted the espressos in the little European cafes and could almost smell the sterile medicinal world in the English hospital. It would be home abroad, a new start, and for months ahead he counted down the days—until she came back into his life.

He had always yearned for her, the way true love continues to haunt the heart long after a relationship has ended, but every exasperating feeling rushed toward him the day of her graduation party. There she sat, sweet pink flower tucked in her hair. He resisted scooping her up and never letting her go, instead focused on keeping his past at a distance from his present. It worked for about a week or two, until the victim in her won him over. He hated calling her a victim; it is much to the accord of saying someone is weak. Weak isn't even in her vocabulary as she fought like a starving, scared cat backed into a corner. She even pushed back against him as he tried to help ease her burdens, but he didn't mind. He only wanted to build an impossible wall around her so her ex could never get to her again. If she hadn't have recreated her favorite childhood memory of him, his own personal walls may never have fallen. He walked into her adorable little world and melted like an iceberg in the Caribbean. The worst part about it was she literally had no idea what she was doing, toying with him like that. All the while she felt like they were friends, he was merely a protector of sorts; he was so in love with her that he would have more than likely died to keep her safe. He was on the verge of throwing himself into heartbreak head first when time ran out; he packed his bags and found himself roaming

The Purpose

incessantly through the streets of Europe, alone.

Time had never been on his side. Growing up, he watched as other's dreams came true. Other people in his graduating class took to life with great ambition, searching for clues to complete their perfect dream of a puzzle. He was different. He started out slow, hating to leave his father behind. The many years after his mother's death, he still struggled with the look on his father's face when he spoke of her. If he had left right away, he would have left him alone. Instead, he hung back, attending a local university. Science had always been his strong suit; anything with configurations intrigued him.

By his sophomore year, he watched one too many episodes of ER with George Clooney and he took to medicine like a lifeline. He never wanted to see another man suffer from losing his wife the way his father did. She passed from an instant implosion of her brain tumor and time was her worst enemy. Will watched on as the soul center of his world, his mother, died at age thirty-two. She never even had the chance to embrace middle-age. Something in him clicked with all the loss of life, that if he had any fighting chance to watch over and protect those that he loved, it was his personal mission.

It was the same for Audrey's father. She had been so hurt, anger pouring from her eyes, at the idea of him leaving her in the dark about his condition. The truth of it was, the most dignified way a doctor, or any person for that matter, can honor another is to allow them their way of telling those that they love. Even if someone cares for another the way

The Purpose

Will cared for Audrey, little matters more than the relationship between families. He only hated the way she found out. He had often wondered if she volunteered at the hospital to be near him, but regardless, it was that world that helped her heal her heartache. Life becomes real, priorities are straightened and bonds are sealed within the walls of a hospital. No matter the pain he caused her, he didn't regret anything.

She stirred, stretched her arms from underneath the warm comforter and fought to open her sleepy eyes. He reached for her and tucked her curls away from her face. She stretched once more, this time yawning.

"I'm still not used to the idea of you in my bed." She attempted to smile seductively.

He kissed her forehead and lingered to breathe in her shampoo. "You have slept for almost twelve hours, you know?"

She pulled herself up in the bed and looked around his apartment, or rather flat. "Really?" She yawned again. "Has it been that long? How glorious!"

His furnished apartment was tucked on the Eastern side of Norwich, less than a mile from the hotel she had stayed in. Ironic how close they had been all along. The space was surprisingly modern for this district with neat, simple colors and lines. It belonged in a catalogue with silver accents, candlesticks and perfectly pleated curtains. Their bed was a king-sized, cherry wooden sleigh bed of navy sheets with silk silver thread. She stretched her legs out, feeling the cool sheets against her ankles.

The Purpose

"Didn't you sleep the whole time, or have you been creepily staring at me?" She raised an eyebrow.

"Both." He nodded seriously. "I prefer to take mental pictures."

She scooted across the little space between them and pressed her lips to his. He still managed to smell of sweet cologne and a hint of red wine. He was adorable first thing in the morning. She had spent many a night sleeping next to him through the years, but never like this. She ran her fingers through his flattened curls, along his scruffy bearded cheeks and eventually wrapped her arms around him tightly, afraid he was only in her imagination.

He hugged her back, gently running his fingers along her backside. "You know, as much as I love us in this bed right now, I might die if I don't eat something, anything. Feed me some of your low-fat popcorn crisps. I really don't care."

She laughed and then slid herself out of the bed to the bathroom to change. Staring at the sleep lines and smudged mascara on her cheeks, she giddily smiled back at her own reflection. Was she really in England, in bed, in love with Will? She jumped up and down, flinging her blonde curls around in circles. Maybe it was the hours upon hours of sleep, but she had never felt so alive.

* * * *

She stayed in England for five more days before heading back home to Missouri. They toured every site, caught trains to Paris, London and her favorite of all places, Italy. She gorged herself on every type of pasta

The Purpose

and gelato, laughing as her pants grew tighter each day. They drank several bottles of wine, tasting real Italian grapes, and watched sunsets in each other's arms. It was a honeymoon to their romance, no wedding needed yet. She found herself permanently nestled into the crevice of his arm, feeling the strength of him. Everywhere they walked, something on them touched, whether it was their hands, arms linked or even the time she rode on him piggy back style when they walked circles around the Eifel Tower. She couldn't resist kissing his lips mid-sentence, ultimately leading to a passionate kiss that lasted much longer than a moment.

On her final morning, she sealed up the zipper to her overstuffed suitcase, packed with souvenirs for Lacy, Lilly and her family, new tops from Paris and the most amazing historical version of *Little Women* she found tucked away in a Norwich bookstore. Bouncing up and down, she finally got it to zip, and rested upon it, frowning. She wanted to stay forever, at least until Will finished. The thought of waiting to kiss him again for months to a year when he finally came home killed her. Sure, he would visit, he had promised, but he would once more board the plane and leave her behind. He had stroked her cheek the night prior, insisting that she had so many things to distract her now that he would be home before she knew it. Plan or not, their romantic getaway would come to an end, leaving her with desperate images of him slurping spaghetti noodles. She had convinced herself that she didn't need him, but maybe, just maybe, she did.

The Purpose

He kissed her firmly before patting her on the behind with a laugh as she made her way through the airport. Even in humor, he was the most irresistible man she had ever known. She turned, catching his glance, and called out, "No one will ever find a love like ours," through the open sea of people. He pressed his hand to his mouth and sent the final embrace over the passing crowd to her lips before mouthing the word, "Never."

Chapter 18

Fall

"Hurry!" Emma called out from behind the bedroom wall.

Audrey raced in to find her sitting in the middle of hundreds of balloons and curled ribbon.

"What on earth? How?"

"Oh just shut up and help me up. I can barely sit on my own, let alone stand." Audrey pushed balloons away from her legs and untwined the ribbon from around her right ankle. "You never cease to amaze me. One…two…three."

She hoisted her with all her strength and her very pregnant sister rose from the ground in slow motion. She was sweating and irritated at Audrey's mocking face.

"Get over yourself. You know I am proud of you; you don't have to smile all the time." She reached out and pinched Audrey's arm. "There, now let's go get 'em."

The Purpose

Lacy tapped on the door. "You guys okay in there?"

"Peachy," Emma called out. "Just peachy."

"Well, everyone's here. They even have supersized scissors!"

Audrey squealed in delight. It was really happening. Emma and Lacy headed outside to greet those gathering in the street. She waited until she heard the door click behind them before falling to her knees. "Claudia, thank you. Thank you for loving me, believing in me and for giving this dream wings."

Will was due home next week, and although she was heartbroken he couldn't be there, she stood firmly on her own two feet with the women who loved her. Lacy had saved enough for a deposit on her own place and although Audrey begged her not to go, she insisted it was time. Cancer free, she was ready to take care of her baby.

Emma was due any day now, crabby but glowing nonetheless. Her mother stood waiting by her father's side, the sun shining down on her glamorous oversized hat, a gift from Claudia. She clasped her Mary Jane heels and headed out to meet them. Together they stood, pride rippling from one face to the next, holding a bright red ribbon from one end of the group on down.

Her eyes filled with tears as she lifted her hands out toward them. "I love you guys so much," she said, choking on her sobs. "But if I don't stop crying, I will never get through this!"

Mayor Boyd reached a hand toward hers. His grin was flashy, eccentric. "How do you do, Miss? You ready to do this?"

"Now or never." She bypassed his outstretched hand

The Purpose

and wrapped her arms around him. He stood startled as the giddy blonde woman clung to him, finally reaching a hand up to pat her lightly on her back.

She stood next to him, one hand on the giant scissors along with his and waited. The group quieted and a small chirping bird filled the silence. Final leaves were falling from the large oak tree overhead. Audrey took a deep breath.

"Welcome, on behalf…"

"Wait!" Will came running through the street, one shiny black shoe in front of the other, face clean-shaven, eyes alive with excitement. "I need to be a part of this!"

Audrey's face lit up and her tears started again. "He made it," she whispered.

He pulled her toward him, the large scissors squished in between, along with the mayor smashed up alongside them, still holding his half.

"Sorry I'm late," he whispered into her hair. "But I wouldn't have missed this for the world."

He stood alongside her as the mayor started again, saying, "On behalf of the proud city of St. Louis, Missouri, I proudly congratulate Audrey Landrow, new business owner of *Faith House*. Together we can improve our community and celebrate the joy of support and a safe place for the women in need. Welcome and congratulations!"

With that, they sliced through the cherry red ribbon, her family jumping up and down, cheering. Will pulled her toward him, smothering her in kisses. "I am so proud of you," he spoke softly.

In a little less than a year, her world had tipped over,

turned around and finally started. Looking around at all of the people she loved, she felt a tinge of sadness. This was only possible because of the beautiful love of a great friend. When someone believes in the best in someone, even before they discover it themselves, it fills the world with a little more faith.

The *Faith House* would be a place of refuge for so many as it had once been for her. Women could rely on something real for once when nothing else seems possible. Audrey had pulled herself up from beyond disbelief to find strength in her own spirit, something she could surely help other women do. Love is contagious; that is something Claudia had taught her. No matter the intention, if it comes from love, it will surely prevail.

"Hey you." Will slipped his arms around her and nuzzled her neck. "Remember what you told me a few months ago?"

"What's that?" She glanced from her family to his loving eyes.

"You said you had found your way back home." He swiveled her around to the sight of all those who loved her, chatting and laughing in her most special place.

She finished his thought, saying, "And I'll never get lost again."

~THE END~

ABOUT THE AUTHOR

"My soul belongs tucked inside the pages of an extraordinary novel."

Whether reading or writing, Joshlyn Racherbaumer has found the key ingredient to a beautiful life. While enjoying the riches of God's abundant glory, she lives in St. Louis, Missouri, with her very own Prince Charming and her three babies: two kitties and a dog. By day she works in marketing and by night she is enveloped in the written word. A family-focused person, she spends a great deal of her free time with her loved ones and is an avid animal rescuer.

*For your reading pleasure,
we invite you to visit our
web bookstore*

WHISKEY CREEK PRESS

whiskeycreekpress.com